YES, SIR

YES, SIR

EROTIC STORIES OF FEMALE SUBMISSION

EDITED BY
RACHEL KRAMER BUSSEL

CLEIS
PRESS

Published in the United States by Cleis Press Inc., P.O. Box 14697, San Francisco, California 94114.

Printed in the United States.
Cover design: Scott Idleman
Cover photograph: Roman Kasperski
Text design: Frank Wiedemann
Cleis Press logo art: Juana Alicia
First Edition.
10 9 8 7 6 5 4 3 2

Contents

INTRODUCTION: READY TO SAY YES (SIR)

When I started working on *Yes, Sir,* I didn't expect the title phrase to be taken as a literal motto, but more as a call to arms (or rather, to surrender one's arms) for submissive women who seek out dominant men. I intended *Yes, Sir* and its companion volume *Yes, Ma'am* to be the bottoms' answers to my previous collections *He's on Top* and *She's on Top*, to showcase our fantasies, desires, and deepest wishes. I wanted those of us who love to be tied up, spanked, blindfolded, bound, or "used" for another's pleasure, to tell it like it is, to explore why and how we get off in these ways, and the authors presented here gave me what I was looking for—and more.

Here you'll find all sorts of women for whom their own personal Sirs (or Masters or Daddies) hold the reins to their erotic pleasure. For them, saying yes (or a bratty, defiant no for which they'll be duly punished) is as powerful as a good, hard smack on the ass. They give up control in all kinds of ways, from letting their doms decide who they'll fuck to when they'll come,

to which color panties are acceptable—and which aren't. In one
of these stories (you'll have to keep reading to figure out which
one), playing at Sir, having your lover become the Sir of your
dreams when real life may dictate otherwise, lets the two play-
ers take their kink to a whole new level.

Some are old pros at BDSM, and have had many masters,
while for others, the language of domination and submission is
a novelty. They may not know exactly why they thrill to being
told what to do, but they know for sure that they like it, as in the
case of the newbie in "Sitting on Ice Cream." D. L. King's Libby
overcomes her natural shyness in "The Day I Came in Public,"
proving that the very acts she first scoffs at are ones that give her
no end of delight. It's almost as if the doms who enter their lives
see the potential for submission in these women, and want to
bring it forth for their own naughty motives, along with making
the women come harder than they ever have before.

The inherent power dynamics of the classroom are brought
to light in Donna George Storey's "Dear Professor Pervert," a
story in which, once official class time ends, the real learning
(about everything from masturbation to butt plugs) begins, as
well as in Lisabet Sarai's "Body Electric," wherein a prominent
professor shows a colleague his very intriguing "apparatus." In
Sommer Marsden's "In the Corner," the man who first introduced Amelia to kink lures her away from her current "nice
guy" date.

These women aren't pushovers by any means. They make
rules and negotiate with their masters, though sometimes they
also get off on being pushed just a little too far by men they
know they can trust. In "The Art of Darkness," Alison Tyler
writes, "Once Killian understood my fear, his mission became
not to save me from my phobia, but to exploit it, every chance
he could." She objects, but when she finally surrenders, she

experiences a whole new world, where a blindfold is the path to ecstasy. And the woman who lets her man dictate her meals in Elizabeth Coldwell's delicious "Lunch"? Well, she knows exactly what she's doing. "I could go home and just tell Michael I'd done as he instructed. But he would know. He always knows when I try to disobey him, however careful or sneaky I try to be." In other words, she's not doing what he says simply because he says it, but because something inside her gets off on obeying. So too in Shanna Germain's story, the protagonist makes an active choice to go where her inner ache to submit compels her: "'Follow,' he said. Something in me resisted, but the power of his voice, the way he walked away from me as though he knew I would trail after him, made it so I couldn't say no." And the woman getting fucked on the sofa in Maddy Stuart's short, sexy tale flinches at the words *slut* and *whore,* even as her body responds to them. This duality, with the brain protesting but the blood rushing to the surface, is also part of the thrill of submission, especially for strong, powerful women.

These writers make clear just how much their characters get off when they say "Yes, Sir," whether literally or figuratively. Sure, they may be doing their masters' bidding, but the masters are often doing the subs' bidding, in their own way, as well, making them ache, moan, quiver, and, yes, come. They know just how to draw out their subs' pleasure (and pain), how to make the most of a woman whether she's on her knees, or bent over, or at her computer waiting for the next command. They know that denial, temptation, and frustration can be the most arousing acts of all. They know that, as Teresa Noelle Roberts puts it, "The Power of No" can often be just as hot as the power of yes.

Gwen Masters asks in her title, "How Bad Do You Want It?" I turn that question over to you, dear reader. How bad do you want to be bound, gagged, spanked, or slapped? How bad do you want to have your hair pulled, your nipples clamped, your body strung up? How bad do you want to pant, gasp, scream, and squirm? How bad do you want to turn over some part of yourself to a man just dying to strip you bare and take you somewhere you've never been? I don't know about you, but I want all of those things, very much, and, I'm thankful to say, I (and you) have them all right here. Just turn the pages, and be prepared not to get up for a good long while.

Rachel Kramer Bussel
New York City

THE ART OF DARKNESS

Alison Tyler

Killian said, "Put your hands over your head."

I obeyed immediately, the "Yes, Sir," coming quickly to my lips.

He clicked on the cuffs, looped the silver chain over the hook above our mattress, then looked down at me. His pale green eyes seemed to glow, like jade lit from within, and I could tell he wasn't finished, even though sometimes all he needs is to see me cuffed. Sometimes that's all it takes. But tonight, he had more serious plans.

"Spread your legs," he said next, and I followed the command, just as quickly. "Yes, Sir," punctuated the movement of my slim thighs parting on the cobalt-blue satin comforter. He bound my ankles securely with leather thongs attached to hooks on the bed frame, and I reveled in the pull on my muscles, the ache that had started already.

"Mouth open," Killian instructed, dangling the bright red rubber ball gag in front of me, and I parted my lips and lifted my neck to make it easier for him to fasten the buckle beneath my heavy, silver-streaked hair. The rubber tasted bitter, an obscene flavor I found oddly pleasing.

"Close your eyes," Killian said finally, and *that's* when I started getting scared.

Killian, I would have said, if the gag hadn't been in the way. *Killian, please.*

The words sounded clear in my head, but as I could no longer speak, I hoped my eyes spoke loud enough for me. Hoped he understood what I was saying. Of course he did. He knew me well enough by now. In fact, I had no doubt that he'd put in the gag before giving this instruction for the sole purpose of seeing if I'd obey.

"*Close your eyes,*" he repeated, his voice sterner now, and I drew in a deep breath through my nose, but kept my eyes open.

I felt as if I'd never blink again.

When Killian had first suggested a blindfold, I'd balked. Worse than that, I'd safeworded, to his total shock. "Jasmine," I'd said quickly.

"What did you say?"

"Jasminejasmine*jasmine.*" The words were strung together in my haste.

"You do everything else, Greer," he murmured, surprised at my instantaneous and—in his view—negative response. "You willingly wear the cuffs, the collar, the chastity belt. You bend over for my cock anytime. Anywhere. Why won't you wear a blindfold?"

I shrugged, unwilling to say, while he continued.

"That's practically vanilla sex. Women who read *Ladies' Home Journal* use blindfolds."

I wondered where he got that last bit of information. He didn't know any women who read *Ladies' Home Journal*. But I understood his point. Blindfolds were almost comically acceptable now. I could have walked into any one of my friends' apartments and found one tucked in a dresser drawer. Who *wouldn't* wear a blindfold?

That was simple: me.

"You've let me drip wax on you, let me use anal beads the size of walnuts. We own a crop, a flogger, a studded paddle, and a cane. What's up with a blindfold?"

I hadn't wanted to admit the truth right away. What if he thought I was some sort of freak? But Killian simply wouldn't let go of the concept.

He held the offending item before me, let the soft velvet fabric slide against my skin, and I squirmed away as if he were using electroshock therapy. (But the truth is that I *would* have let him use electroshock therapy. I'd have let him use one of the violet wands over me before I would allow him to fasten the dreaded fabric over my eyes.)

Still, all I could think to say was, "You won't make fun of me?"

He gave me a look.

"Sir," I added quickly. "You won't make fun of me, Sir, will you?"

"Greer," he crooned. "Don't you trust me?"

"Yes, Sir." If I didn't trust him, then none of our dirty little games would have worked. But I needed reassurance. Because I'd been dreading this day from the start.

I'm a smart girl. I'd understood that eventually Killian would want to try some sort of sensory deprivation, something different than cuffs or bindings. So, yes, I'd known this conversation was coming, but that hadn't made the arrival any easier.

"Then what's the fucking problem?"

Ah, Jesus. I had to say, had to spill my secret. My darkest secret. Or, rather, my secret about the dark. "I'm afraid," I said finally.

"That I'll do something to you?" he asked, incredulous. "That I'll hurt you in some way? In some way you wouldn't like, I mean." A dark chuckle there, because we both knew exactly how much I liked it when he hurt me. His hand, or his belt, or the braided leather of his crop landing cleanly where he wanted each blow. He knew precisely how wet I got simply from the *threat* of having any one of his favorite devices used on my bare skin. He also knew that I had complete faith in him to take care of me, to know my boundaries, to never take me past where I was willing to go.

"I'm not afraid that you'll hurt me," I insisted. "I'm just scared."

"Scared of *what*?" Killian had pressed, unwilling to let me get away with a simple "scared." Which meant I'd have to either confess, or get over my fear. And I saw no way of doing so. Not after living with the phobia my whole life.

"I'm scared of the dark."

It was a child's fear, yes, but that didn't make the fear any less real.

I don't believe I'd ever been in absolute blackness. Throughout my childhood, I slept with a light on, and not just some little princess-pink twinkling nightlight, but a sturdy desk lamp outfitted with a vibrant one-hundred-watt bulb. In college, I'd stay awake each evening reading until my roommate fell asleep, and then I'd pretend to fall asleep myself with the light still on. When living on my own, there was never a problem. I could light the whole place as brightly as the Las Vegas strip if I chose, and nobody would say a word.

Dating wasn't an issue, either. Men seemed charmed, seriously delighted, when I said I liked to keep the lights on during sex. So many women prefer to hide their bodies in blackness. And I rarely had my lovers over to spend the whole night. If one wanted to, I'd leave the hall light on, "for my cat," so that I was never in total darkness. This is what I'd done with Killian. Up until now, anyway. But now I had to fess up.

Because Killian wanted more than simply to stay the night.

He wanted to move in with me.

Once I confessed, Killian's response wasn't at all what I expected. He smiled. A genuine smile, lifting his lips, touching the corners of his eyes. And then he started to laugh. As if he understood. As if it all made sense now.

I felt relief wash over me. But it was a misplaced sensation. I'd thought that he would drop the concept of blindfolding me, that he would be satisfied with the games that I could easily play. All of those other kinky interactions that we shared. What was so exciting about a blindfold, anyway? There were a million other ways that Killian and I could entertain ourselves. He had a toy chest filled with deviant devices. Plenty to keep Killian's hands, mind, and cock well stimulated.

That's what I thought, anyway.

But I thought wrong.

Once Killian understood my fear, his mission became not to save me from my phobia, but to exploit it, every chance he could.

"Close your eyes," he'd say when I least expected to hear the words. We'd be driving somewhere, about to enter a tunnel, perhaps, and he'd taunt me with the command.

"No, Killian. Come on…"

"You'll earn a spanking if you don't behave."

I could happily agree to that. I like being spanked. I hate the dark.

Late at night, I would occasionally hear a telltale click, and I'd wake up in a shuddering panic, realizing he'd shut off my safety light. I'd scramble spiderlike across the mattress, all sprawling limbs and trembling fingers, fumbling in my haste to turn the light back on, and Killian would watch me the whole time. Head tilted, as if storing up the information to use sometime in the future.

Sometime in the very near future.

Sometime like tonight.

"Close your eyes," Killian said again.

I tried to beg now, even with the ball gag in place. "Please, Killian," words which I heard in my head, but which were incomprehensible around the gag. Mere slurring sounds, rather than an actual sentence, but words that I knew my man understood plainly.

"Do it," Killian insisted.

And I shook my head, wondering what that would mean to Killian, wondering what my disobedience would do to him.

In the past, we'd arrived at this precipice, and stopped. It was almost as if Killian thought that someday, I'd simply obey. At some point, if he asked often enough, if he told me often enough, I would get over my fear, or swallow my fear, for him.

But phobias don't work like that.

I once worked for a woman who was afraid of balloons. Beyond afraid. They sent her into serious chest-tightening panic attacks. And you might think this is an easy fear to simply avoid. Stay away from children's birthday parties, right? But now that you know about this fear, pay attention to the world. There are balloons *everywhere*—helium balloons tied to the dry cleaner's sign, outside of the car dealership, heralding one grand opening or another. She'd cross the street to the other side, or drive blocks out of her way, to avoid the ones she knew. But when balloons arrived in her world unexpectedly, she would take an emergency Xanax and call her doctor.

Why was she afraid of balloons? She never said. In the office, we had our guesses. Something to do with pregnancy, with being all puffed up. Or possibly a fear of the unexpected. Of loud noises. Of pops.

Fears don't have to make sense, to play by anyone's rules.

Not even Killian's.

"Tonight's the night," he said, staring at me. "We'll go slowly. We'll take our time. But I want you to know that by the end of the evening, you'll understand."

Why had he gagged me? How could I safeword?

"I'm not going to blindfold you," he continued. "You'll do it yourself. See? If it's too frightening, too difficult, you can just open your eyes again. You won't need to give a safeword."

It was as if he'd read my mind.

"Try," he said again. "For me, Greer. Do it for me."

He had attempted to understand before. I shut my eyes every night, after all, right? To go to sleep. How was that any different?

Because, I'd tried to explain. *Because* it is. Just shutting my eyes for the hell of it, for the sole point of plunging myself into darkness—*that* was a completely different sensation than closing my eyes to sleep.

"Come on, baby," he said. "It's like the first time we had anal sex. Remember? I let you back up onto me. I let you take it inch by inch. That's what I'm asking you to do now. Get used to the feeling of me touching you, kissing you, playing with you while your eyes are closed. Then we can move forward. Then we can try all sorts of things. You *do* trust me, baby, don't you?"

I did. That was the truth.

But the first time I shut my eyes for him, I opened them up immediately.

"That was half a second," he said, laughing.

I tried again, shutting my eyes, my whole body taut. Killian set a hand on my leg and I opened my eyes once more.

"A bit longer this time," he said, "but I think you can do better than that. Try harder, doll. Try for me."

That's what the whole game was about, wasn't it?

Obeying him. Pleasing him. And by pleasing him, pleasing myself. I closed my eyes, and I tried to focus on the sensations that immediately flooded over me. It was as if Killian could tell when I started to give in, when the magic of being a sub began to work through me. He touched me so softly, so gently, and I shuddered and almost opened my eyes—*almost*, but didn't.

He put his hands on the insides of my spread thighs, and his fingertips began to tickle me, sweetly, so that my body would have squirmed away had I not been so completely bound.

My breath came in great shuddering gasps, but I kept my eyes shut. I don't know how I managed to do so, but I did. But then he brought his mouth to the split of my body and licked me firmly, and immediately my eyes opened. The pleasure making me forget the game. Making me fail.

"Good girl," he said. "Let's try a little longer."

Once more, I put my trust in Killian. I took a deep breath in through my nose, as if preparing for an underwater spring, then closed my eyes, and let myself go. Killian was between my legs once more, licking me, his fingers spreading apart my pussy lips. I shivered at his touch, but I was aware now. I kept my eyes shut tight, knowing that if I wanted him to continue, I had to obey. And then, right when I felt that I had got the knack of this, Killian surprised me.

He stopped his licking tricks, and moved on the bed. My eyelids fluttered for a moment, so that his actions appeared almost in strobe-effect. He was coming closer, and I had an idea what he was going to do, but I didn't squirm. Fear spread through my body, but this time, rather than fight it, I let it in.

The blindfold fit over my head, and I started, but then kept myself in check. Not only did the gag prevent me from talking, but a change had started to overtake me. This time, the blackness enveloped me completely. When I peeked through my shut lids, I could see nothing. Fear continued to creep through me, but Killian had a way to keep that fear away.

He slid back between my thighs, and this time I felt his cock, so hard, so ready, poised to enter. Then he slid inside me, and I bucked and moaned. Overwhelmed by the sensation of drifting. Of being carried away.

The blackness helped. The darkness made everything different. Stretched out each sensation, as if we were fucking in the middle of the night, in an open field, surrounded by a black, inky sky.

Why had I fought this for so long? This was simply the natural progression. Being bound. Being gagged. And being blinded. But somehow, in the dark, I found my way. Somehow, in the dark, I could see.

Killian drove in deep, and I lifted my hips as high as I could. There wasn't much give in the bindings, but I did my best to let him know with my body how good he was making me feel. His fingers strummed over my clit, and I started to come. Seeing stars, seeing gold. Seeing beauty in blackness.

Who would ever have thought?

With a final thrust, Killian came, and I shuddered all over and came with him, my safeword the furthest thing from my mind.

DEAR PROFESSOR PERVERT

Donna George Storey

Assignment #4: Bring yourself to orgasm without using your fingers, hands, vibrator or other sex toy. Record the experience in your Masturbation Journal, following the usual guidelines. Your last submission showed much improvement—the use of imagery and language was excellent. Keep up the good work. Sincerely, Professor Pervert.

I click CLOSE MAIL and smile. The professor probably thinks this one's going to be a challenge, but I already came up with the answer ten years ago—back when I was in college the first time around. Doing a "no-hands" is actually pretty easy. You bunch up your pillow, straddle it like a lover, and work your hips just so while you play with your nipples. It feels great, plus you get a good core workout.

Of course, I'll be required to confess that I'm bringing prior experience to the assignment, but I figure I can make up the lost points with an extrasteamy journal entry. I was pretty inhibited at the beginning, but the professor's right. I am improving.

I stroll over to the linen closet and take out a towel. Today I have about two hours to complete the assignment and write it up. If I don't have my paper in his inbox by 9:00 p.m. London time, there will be "penalties." Afterward I'll have just enough time to shower and get to campus for my real summer school class, The Twentieth Century British Novel.

I pull off my oversized T-shirt and shimmy out of my panties. *Totally naked, above and below.* That's what I'll write under *What were you wearing?* in the journal.

Next I fold the pillow and wrap it in the towel. I always get very juicy when I'm doing it for the professor. I stretch out on the bed and push the pillow between my legs, resting on my elbows to allow for good access to my breasts, which *dangle like cones of white wisteria, tinted tender pink at the tips.* The professor will love that. He specializes in the Romantic poets and is partial to natural imagery.

I note the time on the clock above my bed, then cross my arms and begin to caress my breasts, my right hand cupping the left tit, my left hand stroking the right. My nipples feel soft and satiny and more sensitive than when I'm lying on my back, my usual position for self-pleasuring. I push my hips into the pillow, grimacing at the nubby texture of the towel against my tender slit. Maybe this isn't the answer after all?

Think, Tina, think. The rest will come.

It's the professor's voice, smooth and deep, guiding me ever onward to new achievements.

I close my eyes and think.

A man steps from the melting red shadows behind my eyelids and stands at the bottom of my bed. His gaze is fixed on my naked ass. I can feel it, as bright and hot as a spotlight. I squirm involuntarily and that sweet, achy sensation of longing floods my belly. What is he thinking and feeling as he watches a horny slut masturbate just for him?

I begin to hump the pillow with slow, rhythmic thrusts. I can make out the man's face more clearly now—the lush, curly brown hair, the wire-rim Russian Revolutionary glasses. He is young—only two years older than I am and not even tenured yet—but he has enough of a snotty academic air that I yearn to rub away at that smug composure with every jerk of my hips. I want him so jealous of this pillow that he'll start begging me to let him take its place between my legs.

I pause mid-thrust and sigh. The sensation still isn't intense enough to bring me off. It might work if I could use my fingers to spread my labia and get direct friction on my clit, but of course, the assignment specifically forbids it.

I know you have it in you, Tina. Push a little harder. Show me how naughty you are deep inside.

"Yes, Professor," I whisper, into the air. I do want him to see me; not just my flesh, but my darker, deeper places.

The room shifts; the morning light filtering through the curtains turns to a harsh fluorescent buzz. Steel prison bars bisect the room, and my bed becomes a cot covered with a rough, gray blanket. I'm still humping a pillow, my bare buttocks aimed straight at the bars, but the audience has expanded tenfold. A carefully selected squad of prisoners has been brought here to watch an oversexed girl get herself off without using her hands. It's not clear if this is a reward or a punishment for these hardened criminals. I know the guards are sadists. They've told me that if I don't come this way in twenty minutes, the whole crew of correctional officers will get to fuck me on the sagging sofa in their employee lounge in ascending order of cock size. They warned me with a leer that the biggest one, Harry the

Horse, has a dick that would put a baseball bat to shame.

The stakes are definitely higher now.

I rock my hips faster against the damp towel. The prisoners' eyes bore into my flesh. They're bad guys, lifers. They haven't had a woman in decades, and their soft howls of frustration ricochet off the concrete walls. With a fearful glance over my shoulder, I see their huge, swollen cocks are protruding from their flies. Some pump themselves frantically, heedless of the grinning guard. One pushes himself through the bars, fucking the air, as if he can enter me that way if he tries hard enough.

"Boys, you've got five minutes to finish your business, then it's back to your cells," the guard barks. Then his voice turns to sugar with a touch of poison. "You, too, sweetheart. Five minutes or you know what we've got waiting for you."

"I've seen enough assholes in this joint. Make her flip over and show us her cunt," a hoarse voice grumbles.

I hear the crack of a fist landing on flesh, a bellow of pain.

"What you see is what you get," the guard growls.

The men moan and grunt like beasts as they hurry to empty their balls. My head is bursting with lewd sounds, the rasp of dick flesh being rubbed in spit-moistened fists, the rhythmic knocking of hips against the bars that keep me cruelly out of their reach.

One man stands back, eyes narrowed, arms crossed, his fly firmly zipped. He is watching me, but he's also watching them watching me. It's the professor. Even in this place, as far away from twining ivy as you can get, he's still the one in control.

My nipples are as hard as little pebbles now. When I flick them with my fingers, electric jolts jump straight to my pussy. I'm gyrating like a stripper, sliding my cunt down over the pillow, then jerking back up, like my ass is tethered to a spring. Though I'm usually quiet when I masturbate, I realize I'm

making sounds, too: deep grunts and harsh bellows to harmo-
nize with the *bang-bang* of the headboard against the wall. But
I'm going to make it in time. I can feel the orgasm begin to
grow, a throbbing knot in my gut. And the prisoners are right
there with me. With a collective groan, they shoot their wads
through the bars, spraying my ass with a sizzling fountain of
spunk. The odor fills my nostrils, hay mixed with something
harsh and tinny; the nastiest, naughtiest smell on earth. It's all I
need to push me over the edge. I ride the pillow like a bucking
bronco, screaming myself hoarse as I climax, each contraction
harder and sweeter than ever before.

As the spasms fade to a flutter, I check the clock. Length of
session: twenty minutes from start to finish. I collapse facedown
on the bed and listen to my pounding heart. So far, so good, but
this is just the beginning. It's never really over until the professor
gives me my grade.

"Isn't that Professor Perkins over there? And you've got his table, Tina. Lucky bitch."

Pam and I had a lot in common. We were both education
majors with a minor in English lit; we both worked weekends
at Chez Jacqueline. Of course, she was twenty-one. I was eight
years older and far too worldly-wise to gush over an attractive
young assistant professor.

"Those must be his parents," I said, eyeing the other members
of his party: a slim, well-dressed older woman and a gray-haired
guy who looked more or less like the professor with thirty years
on him. Chez Jackie's was the best restaurant in town and we
often waited on our teachers and their families. I was curious to
see how Perkins would act when he was off duty. In class he was
affable but no-nonsense—forget about getting an extension on
a paper from him.

To my surprise he was positively charming in the candlelit glow of the dining room. He remembered my name and introduced me to his folks with a jaunty, "Tina's without question my best student this semester."

"I know Pam gave you a free dessert when you said that to her last week, Professor, but I'm a tougher nut to crack." I grinned at his dad, who winked back.

"Damn. Because this time it's actually true," Professor Perkins joined right in.

Mom smiled, too, and did a little back-and-forth glance between her son and me that made it clear the professor wasn't currently attached, but Mom was hoping he might find a nice girl soon and she might possibly be yours truly. Which almost made me laugh out loud because I was far too busy getting my life back together to waste time lusting after my professor. Okay, so I did occasionally let my mind wander during class. I'd picture the professor naked and try to guess what his cock looked like erect. Long and slender or thick and florid? Ramrod straight or curved to the left as any P.C. professor's should be? Once or twice I even imagined what it would be like to ride him and watch his face as he came. But I did that with every professor, including the old silver-beards and—during really boring lectures—even a few of the women.

But I should've remembered that Mom always knows best.

I was heading back to the kitchen with a tray of dirty plates when Professor Perkins stepped out of the hallway by the restrooms.

"Excuse me, I know you're busy," he stammered. "But I wanted to let you know I turned in the final grades for your class yesterday."

My stomach did a somersault. Why would he look so nervous unless he had bad news? Yet I'd gotten an *A* on the midterm and very complimentary comments on the final paper: *Your argument is tight and compelling, the writing smooth and flowing—a true pleasure to read.*

The professor smiled as if he read my thoughts. "Don't worry, you did very well. I mentioned it because I'm now ethically allowed to ask if you'd like to get together for coffee or something."

Could it be that while I was fantasizing about Professor Perkins naked, he was returning the favor? Maybe I'd get to see what his cock looked like after all.

"Thanks, Professor. Actually, a bunch of us usually go over to the tapas place for a drink after work around eleven. You're welcome to join us tonight—if your mom and dad give you permission."

He blushed—I was starting to like this shy suitor side of him—but recovered quickly and gave me a grin. "I'm sure I can talk them into relaxing my curfew tonight. After all, there's no school tomorrow. See you later, then, Tina."

I had to admit I felt a little thrill as I watched him stride back to his doting parents. Professor Perkins had me in his power all semester. Now I was turning the tables.

Or so I thought.

> *Assignment #5: Go to the woman-friendly adult store south of campus. Ask a saleswoman for advice on anal toys. Confess your level of experience—beginner, dabbler, veteran ready for a challenge? Purchase the item she recommends as well as a bottle of lubricant. When you return home, insert the toy in your anus and masturbate. Record the experience in your Masturbation Journal, following the usual guidelines. Your last assignment earned A for the journal entry,*

which was nicely paced with evocative imagery. How-
ever, I gave you a B- for practical execution. The point
of these exercises is for you to attempt something you
haven't tried before. I expect you to obey this rule
in the future. If you accumulate enough demerits, it
will be necessary to discipline you appropriately. Sin-
cerely, Professor Pervert.

Ah, yes, Assignment #5. That's why I'm here in this strange pose: sitting on my bed with my back against the headboard, my legs spread wide. It's the only position that lets me keep the butt plug in place while I diddle myself.

Naturally, I bought the beginner's size, a flesh-colored silicone gadget about the size of my ring finger with a bulge in the middle like a swollen knuckle. The bottom flares out into a rectangular base to keep the device from slipping all the way inside. That's what the butch-looking saleswoman at the sex store explained to me. Fortunately, buying the thing was not as embarrassing as I had feared. The woman was so nonchalant, it was like we were discussing lipstick instead of anal sex toys. That is, except at the very end when she handed me the brown paper bag and said, "Enjoy!" with a big grin as if she could see exactly what I'd be doing with my purchase before the afternoon was through. I blushed beet red and rushed out of the store.

To be honest, I probably do make as lewd a picture as any-one could imagine. I'm dressed in the scarlet waist cincher and thigh-highs I bought for Assignment #3, which only accentuate all the bare, juicy parts of me. The air brushes my exposed pussy like cool fingertips, and my nipples are standing out stiff and red. Yet I can't say I'm all that turned on by the assignment so far. For one thing, I'm not sure I bought the right size plug. It was definitely a challenge pushing it inside me—I was poking the slippery, lubed-up thing around my butt crack for a full min-ute—but now that it's there, I can hardly feel it. I'm more excited by the idea that I did this naughty thing just for the professor.

Not that he's here to see me. Yet.

I close my eyes and take a deep breath. Suddenly the summer sunlight fades to a single green-shaded lamp glowing in the au-tumn dusk. I'm sitting on a leather sofa in the same slutty getup, legs open, asshole impaled on a strange little silicone bowling pin. Across from me sits the professor in a wingback chair, flanked by tall bookcases jammed with erudite tomes. With his eyes alone he issues the command: *Touch yourself, Tina. For me.*

My hand dips between my legs. I start to strum. My finger makes a rude clicking sound in the wet folds, and I blush, know-ing he hears and sees it all.

"Are you enjoying this?" he asks, his voice as soft as a silk scarf trailing over naked flesh.

"Yes, Professor," I admit shyly.

"Just 'yes?' That's a vague answer," he snaps. "I want you to be specific about what you find enjoyable. Is it that X-rated toy you shoved up your ass so greedily or the fact that I'm watching you masturbate?"

My throat constricts with shame, but I manage to croak out an answer. "Both, Professor."

"Indeed? I must say I'm enjoying myself as well. But I think we're both disappointed you bought the small one. Next time I want you to get one of the long, fat monsters that made you cringe when you saw them on the shelf. While you're at it, get yourself a big dildo—with veins and a suction cup that sticks to a chair so you can ride it. And another one for your mouth, too. You'd like that, wouldn't you, to be all filled up in every empty, aching hole?"

"Yes, Professor," I whisper. That's the only answer I can ever give him, but in truth I'm not sure I agree. No plastic cock—no matter how huge or swollen—can satisfy me as well as his hot, probing gaze.

"Shall I send you back to the store right now to tell that dyke you're enjoying your timid little butt plug very much, thank you, but you crave something bigger and nastier?"

My heart leaps in my chest. "No, please. I'll do anything for you here in your office, but please don't make me do that, Professor."

He laughs softly. "Your cunt muscles contract very nicely when you're frightened. Which gives me an idea for something we can do here to remedy the situation. At my command, I want you to squeeze your muscles around the toy as tightly as you can and hold it until I tell you to release. Will you do that for me?"

"Yes, Professor," I gasp, my buttocks slipping on the leather of the sofa, already slick with my sweat and juices.

"All right then. Squeeze."

I clutch the butt plug, panting softly. I'm starting to ache back there, but the professor only watches me squirm, silently, for what seems like an eternity. Finally he deigns to utter the words I'm desperate to hear.

"You may release."

I breathe out. An intense tingling sensation radiates from my asshole, up through my torso, and down through my shivering thighs. My jaw drops open and I utter an involuntary moan of pleasure.

"Spread your legs a little wider," he orders coolly. "It makes your pussy lips push out so I can see your hole. You're so slick and swollen today, Tina. I think anal play agrees with you. Once more now, squeeze..."

I grip the toy again, gritting my teeth.

"...and release."

The professor is definitely onto something. My asshole's on fire, the flames shooting higher, licking at my throbbing clit. My finger dances over my stiff little girl-cock sticking out shamelessly, all hard and hungry for the professor to see. I'm going to make it. I'm going to come in front of him with this obscene rubber toy jammed up my ass.

"May I...have...an orgasm, Professor?" I'm too distracted by the sensations to remember if this was part of the assignment.

"Of course, Tina, I always like to see my students bring their work to a satisfying conclusion. I would indeed like you to come—but only at the precise moment I give the order. Is that understood?"

"Yes, Professor." I obediently slow my clit finger to coasting speed. But will my cunt submit as easily to his command?

"Come for me, Tina," he tells me. "Now."

With a grunt, I attack my clit with frantic jabs and squeeze the toy with all my might and—oh, God, it's happening—a wave of burning heat fans through my belly, erupting from my throat in a series of barking cries, as my back bangs against the headboard and my anus milks the butt plug in helpless, rhythmic spasms.

When it's over, I slide down onto the bed and pop the toy out, wrapping it in a waiting tissue. Total time for the session: thirty-five minutes. In my journal entry, I'll tell the professor about his "help" of course, but I'm not sure words will do justice to the quality of my orgasm—a detailed description of which is a strict requirement for each assignment. It was definitely different. It seemed to start deeper inside me, a secret explosion tucked back against my spine. Yet there was something else I couldn't quite name, a hint of exotic spice in a familiar sweet. The only way I can really be sure I'll get a good grade is to try it again and take more careful notes.

I laugh to myself. Strange how my lover is thousands of miles away, but I'm having more and better sex than I've ever had in my life.

After our first "date" for drinks, things moved fast with Professor Perkins. After all, I'd already met his parents. Within the week, I saw his cock, too. It was average in length, but thick, and it turned a lovely rosy color when it got hard that made me think of a strawberry Popsicle, my favorite flavor.

Professor Perkins—I was calling him Jonathan by then—was pretty good in bed, too. At first he was slow and careful, as if he were studying my body to get an A in Tina's Sexual Response 101. But soon enough we were rutting like wild animals. After the sex, we had some pretty intense talks, too. Jonathan told me about his romance with a colleague that didn't survive when she left him for a job on the East Coast. I told him why I dropped out of college the first time: to follow my boyfriend, Devon, on his pilgrimage around the world. Our first year together was the most magical year of my life. The next five were the worst. It was all about Devon's drinking until one day I realized I was giving my life to a man who didn't know me, who didn't even see me at all.

"I love to look at you," Jonathan said, stroking my hair. "And I want to know everything about you."

He was certainly saying and doing all the right things. In fact, it all seemed too good to be true. It was. A minute later, Jonathan told me he was leaving for London the following Monday to do research at the British Library and would be gone for six weeks.

Okay, a few dates and a few fucks didn't really give me any claim on him, but I felt deserted by the bastard all the same.

Still the first week apart wasn't so bad. We emailed every day and Jonathan hinted during a Skype call that he'd love to take me hiking around Wordsworth's Dove Cottage in the Lake Country—next summer perhaps. Could a guy get more sweet and Romantic than that?

In fact, it was my dirty mind that led us down a darker, more twisted trail. It all started innocently enough with a naughty dream.

I was lying on the floor of Professor Perkins' office wearing an old-fashioned schoolgirl's kilt and white blouse. The professor himself was stretched out on top of me, but he didn't really have a body. He was just a hot weight pressing me down, making my flesh feel all tingly and melted. I couldn't see his face either, but I felt his hand stroking my cheek and his voice slipping into my ear. *Your final paper was so good it made my cock hard for two weeks straight.*

Which, of course, didn't make any sense. I mean, how could a ten-page paper on "Ode on a Grecian Urn" give anyone a boner for one minute, not to mention two weeks? However, the dream got *me* so turned on, I lay in bed playing with myself and thinking about Jonathan until I had a very wet, loud orgasm. Even after that I was still horny and missing him terribly. That's how I got the idea to send him a provocative email.

In retrospect it was mild stuff. I told him about the dream and how I "pleasured myself" when I woke up. Then I said, tongue-in-cheek, that I was looking forward to August when I could feel his "pulsing manhood" in my "turgid sex."

After I sent it, I was a little worried he'd laugh or be offended, but instead he called and said in that low, syrupy voice guys get when they're shy but turned on at the same time, that he enjoyed my email and was going to send a reply soon.

I couldn't restrain a giggle of triumph. Last spring I never would have imagined I'd inspire Professor Perkins to send me an X-rated email.

But that wasn't quite what I got. The subject line was simply *Comments on Your Essay*. In a formal, professor-ish tone, he told me my paper would be stronger if I gave more context for the self-pleasuring—what I was wearing, how long it took, and which specific techniques I used to reach satisfaction. He suggested I draw my reader into the scene through the use of vivid detail and avoid clichés such as "pulsing manhood." He concluded that my work showed promise, but there was much room for improvement.

My face burning with embarrassment and disbelief, I fired back a reply.

> *Dear Professor Pervert, I didn't realize I was going to be graded on my effort. Maybe you should write out the assignment with a list of guidelines so I can do better next time?*

A few hours later, I found this in my in-box:

> *Assignment #1: Spend at least an hour pleasuring yourself without bringing yourself to orgasm. After one hour, you may enjoy a climax. You'll be keeping a Masturbation Journal that will be graded on style and content. At the top of each entry record the time of day, length and location of session, and what you are (or are not) wearing as the session unfolds. I'm looking for an accurate and thoughtful essay that explores not only physical sensations, but your thoughts, feelings and fantasies while you are masturbating. Fresh images and honesty are key elements of the exercise. The assignment is due within four hours. Late papers will be penalized. Sincerely, Professor Pervert.*

"The nerve!" I sputtered at the computer, shaking with anger. For a minute, I was too worked up over his audacity to notice he'd gotten me worked up in other ways: my panties were soaking wet.

After I got an *A* for the butt plug scene, I was really looking forward to Assignment #6, but instead I received an email as terse as an old-fashioned telegram: *Coming home early, have to run to catch the flight. Can I see you Saturday afternoon? J.*

In spite of my excitement, I spent most of the morning worrying about what I'd say when I greeted him on my doorstep. "Hey, Professor Perkins, thanks again for reading my kinky fantasies about doing sex shows for convicts and sodomizing myself in your office"? Fortunately, conversation was low on our list of welcome home activities. The instant he arrived we were kissing and ripping off each other's clothes and, within about a minute, fucking like crazy.

Now we're twined together in the afterglow, and Jonathan is telling me how much he missed me and how I'm even more gorgeous than he remembered. Not that I don't like the adoration, but it's a bit cliché. Secretly I find myself missing another man, with more exacting standards, who has apparently decided to stay back in London.

As if he's read my thoughts, Jonathan clears his throat. "By the way, I, um, enjoyed your essays very much. I know it would be different in person, but I came up with some new ideas. It's totally cool with me if you'd rather not, but maybe some day we could...?"

My pulse jumps.

"Try Assignment Six?" I whisper.

He nods, blushing.

"I'd like that very much, Professor. In fact, I'd be up for a lesson right now."

His cock stirs against my thigh, and I feel a change in other parts of his body, too—a squaring of the shoulders, a confident lift to the chin. My heart is pounding now, with the power of it. Because I'm the one who's made this happen, with my words and my desire.

"Very well, Tina, I want you to get up and stand by the bed." His voice is slow and smooth, just as I imagined. "No, don't put on your robe, I want to look at you just as you are."

I crawl out of bed and stand before him. I can't meet his eyes, but I feel them, warm and glowing on my bare flesh. I've never felt so beautiful, so *seen*.

"You like to be watched doing naughty things, don't you, Tina? You like to do things no good girl would ever dream of."

"Yes, Professor," I whisper, my voice trembling.

"In fact, you want to masturbate for me right now, isn't that correct?"

"Yes, Professor." I slip an unsteady hand between my legs and start to rub my clit for him. Except this time he really is watching.

"Your reports were excellent, but I must say I'm enjoying the live performance. Now, for our next assignment I'll be asking you to do some new things that circumstances didn't allow before. I will push you, and stretch you, but I know you have it in you to get top grades."

I let out a soft moan. Images swirl through my head: my body bent over his desk in his office on campus, the professor behind me, probing my ass with the lubed-up knob of his dick. Me on my knees, hands bound behind my back as I suck and suck his strawberry Popsicle prick. I know there will be challenges, even humiliations, but any fear is lost in a sweet, soaring hunger to learn more about all the things our bodies and minds can do together.

"I'll try my best, Professor. If I may say so, sir, I'm glad you're back."

"All thanks to you, Tina. You are without question my most inspiring student. Now listen carefully to my instructions. As you know, I will take points off for sloppiness."

The only proper answer is to nod, obediently, but I can't help smiling, too. He is home, my dear Professor Pervert. I can't wait for class to begin.

A NECESSARY CORRECTION

Debra Hyde

Somewhere, somehow, she had said too much. Kiana knows this the instant the wooden clamp touches her tongue. Blindfolded, she had expected the rubber bit or the tube gag, perhaps even her panties, but when the clamp grabs her, she knows she has committed a verbal transgression. As it tightens, she wonders what it was.

First, Gordon had ordered her mouth open. Now, he binds her, hands to feet, like a calf waiting for the brand. He cinches her to the hoist over their bed, pulls it until it draws her limbs into the air and she rests on her back. He leaves her there, appendages pointing to the ceiling, like a naked piece of meat.

And yet, she isn't. The clamp keeps her from falling into the objectified state that comes when she feels like meat. Although she longs for that nirvana, her bizarre grin, made wide by dowels and nuts and bolts, will not allow it. Its intensity does not allow so simple an ecstasy.

But what did Kiana do to deserve this? She had been pleasing to Gordon all evening, demurely moving about the party crowd naked, following Gordon's lead, always at his beck and call. She had kept to his right, a step behind him, her eyes down, her hands clasped behind her back. She had been obvious in her submission, yet understated and graceful. Never once had she attempted to draw attention to herself.

Her tongue throbs now, its circulation compromised by the clamp's fixed grip, a constriction that, while not exactly painful, is not particularly blissful either. If anything, it is sublimely defined. The clamp hugs so strangely that her body floods with endorphins and she floats in ethereal delight, borne on the wings of pleasure perverted.

Gordon had originally designed the clamp as part of a set meant for her breasts, but after a rare instance of impertinence on her part, he had discovered another, highly effective use for it. It had startled her that first time he had applied it, but it had thrilled her as well. Peculiar and overwhelming, it had quickly suspended her in an endorphin haze. Effectively, it had rendered her mute and mentally murky.

She gulps, swallowing spit. It is an exaggerated, gross movement, not the subtle clearing of accumulation that, like eyes blinking, one does without notice. And in the process, a slice of discomfort snaps at her. The small stretch of flesh that connects the tongue to the mouth snags between her lower front teeth. It is a split second sensation, over as soon as Kiana recognizes it. But it always scares her. It always feels as if that slender sliver of flesh will lodge between her teeth, stuck there until ripped free by sheer panic.

The frenulum, Kiana thinks. *It's called the frenulum linguae.*

She thinks it odd that its Latin nomenclature is so closely cousined to that of male genitalia. She wonders if Gordon's anatomical equivalent is stretched tight by an aching erection.

Does he take devious delight when he watches her swallow? Does the sight of her dry, cracked lips surrounding her obvious, inflamed tongue ignite him?

Lips. Labia oris. The mouth is, to Kiana's amazement, the only place where labia and frenulum meet in noncoital unity. *Blow jobs aside,* she adds.

Why she remembers these things under the sway of Gordon's implements, she cannot say. In the fog of endorphins, her mind often wanders into weird places where strange word associations abound. Sometimes, she wonders if extreme bondage is, in its own way, as near a psychedelic trip as one can get without drugs.

She must swallow. Perched on the precipice of disaster yet again, her panic seated in a single, seized breath, Kiana finds resolution in the space of exhaling. Her frenulum remains free.

A shuffle of movement. Gordon, approaching. The bed sinks under his weight, tilting Kiana toward him. Like the flesh catching against her teeth, it is a diminutive sensation, likely imperceptible to Gordon, but she feels the pitch profoundly and gasps. She senses his stare, but his inspection, she knows, will not end with his gaze. It will become tactile, and she braces for it.

His hand closes over the globe of her left breast and squeezes, compressing it so fiercely, she pants guttural gasps. Retreating, fingers go to her nipple and toy with it. Pulling and pinching, they test its give, a luscious attention, and Kiana ignores the uncompromising clamp at her mouth, the mounting ache in her shoulders from prolonged bondage, the strain of the hog-tie on her body. Yearning, she hopes Gordon will continue to grope her; she prays he will linger there. She wishes she could come from this decidedly delectable torment.

But Gordon quits her nipple, dismaying her. His hand travels down the bony terrain of her torso, across the swell of her belly, and settles between her legs. He brushes the lips of her cunt, teases its slit. Kiana trembles. She feels delicate and yielding, like clover in a stiff, summer breeze, its flowers risking the tear of the wind to find the sun's rays.

Intrusion, abrupt and merciless. It shreds her pastorale— penetration robbing her of whatever dignity her brief fantasy has lent her.

It's Gordon's big, thick thumb that pokes about, twisting, turning, and stretching her. Her muzzle does not stop Kiana from begging him to stop this humiliation. She squirms against it, tries to escape it, but the hog-tie holds her fast and when her limbs flare in sudden, stiff pain, she surrenders the struggle.

Gordon's brutishness wins. It always does. And Kiana would not have it any other way. Long ago, she had ceded such power to him, never to contemplate recalling or reclaiming it, always glad to be its thrall, to be its sexual subject. Kiana wants it no other way. Kiana craves it no other way.

His thumb still in her, Gordon leans forward. Kiana feels his breath upon her face and, in the rhythm of his breathing, she hears his arousal. She knows he's rock hard and ready to fuck her. But she also knows this lesson must play out in its entirety.

His tongue brushes against hers, its touch so strong, Kiana flinches. Gordon flicks it about, mimicking a French kiss, but Kiana's tongue is so thick and tender that the kiss feels volatile and shocking. Capriciously, Gordon pulls away from her and rises from the bed. Voided, Kiana pants, her anticipation rising. She knows the lesson nears its apex.

"Do you know what you did?" he asks.

She balks. She doesn't know the answer, only the obvious. She stammers to admit, "I talked too much."

Her words sound, naturally, like she's speaking with an impediment, but somehow Gordon understands her. "To whom? When?"

She shrugs. Although her gesture is abbreviated by bondage, Gordon comprehends this too.

"After your scene."

The scene. Kiana remembers the succulent experience that Gordon had orchestrated at the party. He had strung her up, arms and legs spread wide between two pillars. He had clamped her nipples and strung the length of chain from a ceiling hook, making it supremely taut. It had stretched her pinched nipples obscenely and, peering down at her tits, Kiana had practically drooled at the sight of her nipples treated to this extremity. The pain was delicious, savory, and she had hoped it would last forever.

And then Gordon had whipped her. He had flogged her ass until it reddened and blazed hot to his touch, her back until it was laced with stripes. From behind, he had plied the flogger between her legs, at first soft and slow, just enough to arouse her, to make her want to come. And once she was roused, he had driven her roughly, thrashed her into a frenzy. He had pushed her almost to the peak of orgasm, but not quite. Her nipples screamed, her cunt seeped, and her body anguished, craving release.

Gordon had tossed aside the whip, grabbed her about the waist and jammed his hand between her wet thighs. His thumb sought out her ready nub, sending shudders through Kiana when he found it.

It took only a few swift strokes to make her come—she had been that ready—but Gordon kept at it until a second wave overtook her and anguish turned to ecstasy, willing submission to wilting exhaustion.

Kiana smiles, such as she can, at the memory.

"That was nice," she says, remembering how sweetly she had swayed, bound, in postorgasmic glow.

"Not the scene," Gordon corrected. "Afterward. Someone asked you about the clamps, the nipple play. Remember what you said?"

Afterward...nipple play. Ah, yes!

A couple had asked her what it felt like. Newbies, she remembers. She had had enough wits about her to describe how arousing and amazing the scene was. She had even counseled the couple to start with the gentlest of clamps and work their way up to more challenging ones. She had advised them to take their time experimenting and experiencing. She had said...

She had said, she had said, she...she had babbled. She had monopolized the conversation—had not let the couple get a question in edgewise.

Dismayed, Kiana sighs.

"That couple. I blathered," she confesses, discovering in the process that blathered is a word that does not lend itself to a tongue clamp. Worse, that Gordon understands her nonetheless.

"Yes. Exactly. And what was the penalty the last time you made this error?"

The cane. Ten solid strokes, no warm-up. Kiana's wordless whine says it all.

Gordon presses the cane flat against its starting point, her ass. Kiana quivers; she knows these strokes will be brutal, an absolute test of her endurance. And likely to steer her clear of mistakes in the future. When the cane leaves her skin, she braces for its strike.

The cane sings as it sails toward her ass. Its impact is severe, its sting made worse by the rounded position of her ass. Kiana yelps and sobs follow but they're crocodile tears, insincere and false.

"Ten," Gordon states.

"Thank you, Master," Kiana lisps.

"I will not monopolize the conversation," he adds.

"I will not monopolize the conversation," Kiana struggles to repeat.

The cane strikes again and sends Kiana into a long wail.

"Nine."

"Thank you, Master. I will not monopolize the conversation."

She keens at strikes eight through six, barely able to utter her assigned mantra, and discovers agony in strikes five through three. And she weeps her way through the last two strikes. Tears flow down her face, spill onto the bed, forming a different kind of wet spot.

But the cane has done its job; its fury has ended, and Kiana begins to calm. This necessary correction has come to its conclusion. Gordon fusses at the rigging and frees her from the hog-tie. By default, she expects him to want her stretched out across the bed and ready for a spread-eagle finale, but Gordon surprises her.

"On all fours."

Her limbs complain, but she stoically ignores them and stiffly moves into position. Challenge and chastisement have reduced her to unmeditated obedience; she complies without hesitation or resistance. She is at her deepest level of submission, a place of visceral actions and reactions, a place unthinking and, thanks to the tongue clamp, unspeaking.

Gordon aims his cock at Kiana's swollen slit and, poised to part her, he says, "I don't want to hear a peep out of you." Then, he shoves himself deep.

Kiana lurches, her breath catches in her throat, but she manages to muffle a whimper. Gordon's thrusts skewer her, deep enough to bang against that inner limit, that spot not sweet but wholly sensitive. Kiana knows Gordon is using his cock to test her resolve. She holds her tongue.

Gordon groans. Kiana knows he is staring at the welts on her ass, his handiwork. He gets off on seeing her skin marred by his directives and determinations, on seeing his lust expressed in flagellation's frippery. This fuck, she knows, is all his, meant only for his pleasure, his climax, his satisfaction. His cock has been too hard for too long; the patience of punishment meted out gives way to the haste of lust.

Kiana loves this voracious, selfish rutting. She loves being pummeled, used. Wantonly stupid, she drools. Spittle spills over the clamp, drips from her mouth, but, lost in the intensity of Gordon's fucking, dazed and doped by pleasure's opiates, Kiana is beyond all propriety.

Until Gordon pushes her one last time. His thumb again, this time forcing its way into her ass. He reams her, probing and pulling, pushing her endurance to its limits, all to make her squeal. Finally, unable to withstand this final assault, this cruel penetration, she crumples. Finally, she utters a sound and it shocks her to hear a lowly bleat escape her lips.

But Gordon bellows at the sound of her surrender. Victory throws him into orgasm. He slams his cock into her, balls slapping, and comes. Carnivorous in his climax, he is beastly, spilling into Kiana, pumping with a prowess that diminishes only when he has nothing left to spew.

Drained, he rests against Kiana. His predatory edge fades as his breathing slows from panting, and when he finally pulls himself free of her, his spunk dribbles down her thigh. *My cunt cares no more about propriety than I do*, Kiana thinks.

Gordon draws her to him then and together they collapse into a shared embrace. Briefly, he interrupts it, pulling the blindfold from Kiana's eyes, loosening the clamp from her tongue. Gordon wiggles it free, but not before Kiana cries out again, her tongue tender and sore.

His index finger flies to her lips. "Shhh," he tells her. "Not a sound."

And when he takes her into his arms again, he presses his lips against hers and seeks her tongue. Kiana cannot suppress her reaction, but this time, in Gordon's languid embrace, it is the small sounds of love and adoration that she utters. This time, dominance sated, Gordon does not correct her. Instead, his kiss deepens—and captures Kiana all over again.

THE EDITOR

Amanda Earl

How many rewrites can he possibly demand?" Bettina wondered. "Maybe I should just send the story to a different editor."

She knew she shouldn't keep trying, but she kept thinking that one last effort on her part would satisfy him. And she wanted to satisfy him.

She couldn't put her finger on it, but there was something about the way this editor worked with her. It made her feel...not special. No, that wasn't the right word. Singled out. Yes, that was it.

She wondered about the editor, but she had never even seen the man. Since he spent so much time on her story, she imagined he did so as a labor of love, or perhaps lust.

Her throat went dry and her belly tightened as she let the word roll inside her mouth. Lust. A labor of lust. Maybe reading the story turned him on. The thought of this man, potentially aroused by her story, was enough to make Bettina fidget in her chair. She needed a break.

This was the difficulty with writing erotic stories. The imagination created the itch and the itch had to be scratched. She went into the bedroom and closed the door. She slipped quickly out of her outer clothes, but left her bra and panties on. She opened the drawer of her nightstand and pulled out her clit vibrator, then turned on the DVD player. Naturally, her favorite film was still in place.

She watched as Mr. Wendell Roberts, the head librarian, pulled Chloe, the student with the late fees, over his knee. Bettina turned her vibe on. Roberts raised the woman's short plaid skirt. Bettina spread her legs. Chloe wriggled on his lap and begged him to be gentle. Bettina slid one side of her own white panties down her hip and stroked the smooth white skin of her buttocks. The librarian caressed the round bottom cheeks of his victim, then *smack!* Bettina pushed a finger into her cunt. *Smack!* She used her other hand to move the vibe up to the hardening bud of her clit. *Smack!* The woman was pleading for more now.

The librarian's hand reached beneath her skirt. The camera angle changed and Bettina was given a detailed glimpse of one wet cunt, oozing come. Then the camera moved again as he slapped her hard on the ass. Bettina saw the red hand mark and it sent her over the edge. She humped and humped against the vibrator as the volley of smacks continued, her own moans matching the moans of the willing victim. The vibrator buzzed and throbbed against her clit and she thrust her hips a few last times for the aftershock, squeezing out every last drop of her orgasm. She sighed as the tremors ended. Her clit continued to tremble as the orgasm subsided. She closed her eyes, dropped the vibe and waited for her heart to resume its normal rhythm.

She put on a loose gray robe, then returned to her desk. After a sip of cold water, she penned an email to the editor with an idea. Her throat felt parched as she typed. She gulped another big swallow of water. Her breath rose and fell sharply as she contemplated his possible response. Would it please him? Maybe it would even arouse him. She'd never tried it, but stories involving master and slave turned her on. She'd read a lot of them, so she thought it would make sense.

Her thoughts returning to the porn video she'd just watched, Bettina imagined herself over the editor's lap. His strong hands curled around her firm buttocks, tracing the two dimples resting on either side of the crack of her ass as he prepared her to receive the sharp, stinging pain from the flat of his hand. She was wet again.

This time she didn't turn on porn or return to the bedroom. She threw off her robe, as if he had ordered her to strip. Placing a cushion in the middle of the futon, she lowered herself down to her hands and knees, and pressed her ass out. What would his voice sound like as he commanded her? She spread her legs and pushed herself against the cushion, firmer than most because it was often used for this purpose, and she needed it hard, not too giving. She humped her wet cunt over the cushion and felt the hard nub of corduroy rub against her clit. Her tits stiffened as she imagined the editor's ink-stained fingers squeezing her nipples, turning them red, red for him. Like her ass. Marking her. Using her. She cried out. Her cunt seeped thick come onto the cushion, which now had a wet spot.

The day was flying by. She'd had two orgasms, one walk, no lunch and one great story idea. She checked her email again, but still no word.

She fiddled around and sorted books for a bit, tidying up her desk, but she couldn't figure out what to do with herself. If only he would email, let her know one way or the other.

The ringing of the telephone jarred her out of her increasingly horny thoughts. She picked up the receiver.

"Bettina Brixton?"

"Yes?"

"This is Hamilton Cheevers."

This was him. Her editor. The one she'd never heard from before. And he was calling her. Now.

"Are you there, Ms. Brixton?"

His voice was older. Maybe late fifties or early sixties, it was hard to tell, but the tones were sophisticated, with the trace of an English accent. Nothing extreme. Very educated sounding.

"S-s-sorry," she said, stammering. "Yes. I'm Bettina. So nice of you to call. What made you call me after all this time? Are you calling long distance?"

Suddenly she paused, realizing she was simpering nonstop. She took a deep breath and calmed herself.

"So kind of you to call."

"That's better Ms. Brixton. Your latest idea is spot on. I'm glad you finally understand what I want."

"Thank you. Uh…" She realized she didn't know what to call him.

"Sir. You may call me Sir, Ms. Brixton. And I shall call you Tina."

"Tina. Yes, thank you, Sir."

"Do you have much experience with dominance and submission?"

"Actually, nothing real." She started to squirm, feeling very uncomfortable after her last fantasy involving the editor.

"Well, you'll need to do some research. At least read and perhaps chat with a few people in the lifestyle. I'll email you some sources. Do you think you can have the draft back to me in a week or so?"

"Yes, Sir. Absolutely."

"Excellent. Good girl, Tina. Let's talk again after I've read your latest draft. You've got quite a gift as a storyteller."

Bettina's heart raced.

"Thank you, Sir," she said, stumbling once more in her speech.

"Next time we talk, I do hope you're more comfortable, Tina. Good-bye."

Bettina put the phone down. In her mind she replayed the conversation. Why couldn't she be suave and sophisticated instead of awkward? There was nothing awkward about him. He sounded calm and self-assured, with a commanding voice. Yes, commanding. Her cunt quivered at the thought. She checked her email and found one from him with a list of books, Internet sites and a chatroom recommendation.

She felt like a young girl being taught by an exacting schoolmaster. Her breasts swelled at the thought of his hands on her, but she ignored the feeling, or rather she channeled it into her writing.

She mused about the editor while she worked elements of dominance into her story. She could sense the characters taking shape. The phone interrupted her thoughts. She picked up the receiver and said "Hello," in a rather breathless voice.

"Am I disturbing you, Tina?" said the editor.

"Oh, no. No, Sir. I was just deep into the story." She paused and he said nothing. The air over the phone crackled between them. She cleared her dry throat. "A flogging scene actually." Once more, a long pause on the other end. She held herself still, sat up straight in her chair, stopped playing with her hair.

"Wonderful. Well, don't let me take up your time. I just wanted you to know about the upcoming fetish show and sale in Toronto next weekend. Thought you might want to go. I'll be there representing our publishing house. It would be an opportunity for us to meet."

Bettina's hands grew damp as she grasped the receiver tightly to her ear and she took a deep, calming breath, lowering her voice.

"Really? You want to meet? Oh, I'd like that."

"I'll send you the information then. But I expect that rewrite before then. We can discuss it when you arrive."

"Yes, Sir. I look forward to it. Thanks for thinking of me."

"You're welcome. You sound calmer now. You have a beautiful voice, Tina."

He hung up and Bettina just stared at the telephone, until the recording came on telling her to hang up. She'd pleased him. She let the thought shiver over her body. Soon she would meet him. She tingled with anticipation from her head right to her sopping wet cunt. Now she'd have to redouble her efforts to finish the story. She really needed to talk to people in the lifestyle. She went to the chatroom the editor had mentioned.

Soon she struck up a conversation with Renaissance Master. It wasn't long before they moved into private chat. The conversation moved into a discussion of what he liked about dominance, and it turned her on completely.

You're an intriguing woman, RM typed. *I enjoy a woman who intrigues me. And reward her for doing so.*

Through her loose robe, Bettina's hand glided down to her cunt, and she slipped her fingers inside to feel the sticky juices of her arousal.

Just how would you reward her?

First I'd bend her over my knee...

Mmm, that sounds very rewarding to me. Bettina used one hand to type now as she traced her fingers along her parted sex lips.

To me too. I can't resist a sexy, vulnerable ass over my knee, just begging to be spanked. Do you like that idea?

God, yes. I'd love to be spanked. She leaned close to the

screen, pressing her cunt down onto the black leather chair, moving up and down as she read his words.

And I would love to take you over my knee, but only after you'd served me. Would you like that? Would you like to serve me?

Yes, I dream of serving you.

Are you naked?

No. I have a robe on.

Remove it for me. Bettina threw off her robe and it landed in a gray puddle by her feet.

Yes, Sir. It's off now.

Good girl. Now, while I speak, take your fingers and touch your cunt as if I am touching it. Tease your clit as if my tongue is on it. Imagine you feel the fire of my breath against your skin.

Yes, Sir. Bettina trembled as she followed his commands. He couldn't see her, but she knew that he must be getting aroused by her obedience.

I want you to tell me between 1 and 5 how close you are to coming. Imagine I order you to your knees and tell you to crawl. Number please.

2. Bettina's two fingers moved inside her cunt as she raised it toward the screen and then back down.

I tell you to lie down on your stomach and attach cuffs to your wrists and ankles, then chain you to the bed. You cannot move.

3. Bettina's juices coated her fingers as she pushed her body back down onto the chair.

I walk to the head of the bed. You notice a long red flogger in my hand. I let you smell the leather of its suede lashes. So soft but capable of causing so much pain. You want that pain. One day I'll make you beg for it.

4. Bettina rubbed her clit with her thumb as she humped hard and fast against the chair.

Are you close? Tell me, do you want to come?

Pllleaasse, she typed slowly with one hand while the other was lost inside her frenzied cunt. Her tits were hard and swollen and she needed him to release her.

Come then. Come for me.

Her body shoved itself hard against the chair as the orgasm pounded through her.

5, she typed as the juices flowed down her legs.

Good girl. I hope one day to see you do that for me. Now good night little one. Time for you to dream.

Thank you so much. G'night to you, Sir.

After that encounter, Bettina grew very excited about meeting the editor. Her story glistened with layers of meaning, sensual descriptions, well-honed characters and a sizzling plot. She was very proud of it when she sent it to him. She hoped he would like it.

A few days before the trip, she received a package in the mail. Through the brown paper, it felt yielding. She turned it over and saw the name of the editor on the return address. Her stomach churned and the pulse at her throat beat strongly. With trembling fingers she opened the package. There was a note, but she took no notice at first. Instead her fingers flowed through the dress, made of some light gossamer material, in ash gray. Beneath the dress was a charcoal velvet choker. She wrapped it around her neck immediately and felt a surge of desire course through her so strongly she had to kneel. It was then that she spied the note, written in precise and neat black ink on crisp, white stationery.

> *Your story is perfect, Tina. Please meet me at the Royal York Hotel. There will be a message for you at the desk. Wear the dress, and the collar. No underwear or bra.*

Her fingers slid down to her cunt, so wet, so needy. She couldn't stand it. She dropped to the floor and spread her legs, pressing her fingers against her hard clit and rubbing and rubbing until she came, the collar surrounding her neck. Possessing her. She wanted to serve this man. She had never felt such an urge before, but she knew it was right and he knew it was right. He trusted her to obey him and she would.

She took the train in to Toronto a day early and got her hair done. She also indulged in a Brazilian wax to remove all the hairs on her cunt. She wanted to look perfect for him. As the hair was ripped from her body with the aid of the hot wax, she cried out in pleasure and pain. She imagined his whip on her bare mound, rubbing along her sex lips, covered with her juices of surrender.

The clock marched slowly along as she waited to see him. They'd agreed to meet at seven. She'd gone out for a bit, but couldn't concentrate, so she'd ended up in her room at the Royal York, and she'd done the only thing she could to calm herself. She started to write.

Lost in thought, she was almost late. She changed quickly into her dress and called downstairs for her message. She was to go to Room 332.

She composed herself, ran a comb through her hair, applied her lipstick with trembling fingers and left her room, finding her way to his. Taking a deep breath, she knocked on the door.

"Enter," she heard through the door. The voice was strong and she felt any nervousness evaporate as she walked into the suite.

"Good evening, Tina. You look ravishing."

There he was. Hamilton Cheevers. The editor. He stood there, looking down at her. She let her eyes meet his. His black hair was cut short and neat, with touches of silver at the temples. His blue eyes stared calmly into hers. He smiled briefly, causing a flash of warmth to travel to her stomach and below. Despite the worldly and sophisticated tones of his voice on the telephone, which made him sound like a man in his fifties or early sixties, the editor appeared to be closer to his midforties.

He reached down and took her hand. His hand was not smooth, but calloused. Obviously he was someone who used his hands for manual labor. His fingers had no trace of ink stains, as she'd imagined. She felt his gaze rove down her body.

"You wore it," he said, touching her collar.

"Yes, Sir. Don't I always obey you?"

"So you do. You wouldn't be here otherwise." He motioned to a small table.

"Now let's eat. I want to get to know you further, Tina."

"And I you, Sir." While she was excited, she also felt very calm.

The editor cut a dashing figure in a slate gray suit. Not many men carried off suits well anymore, but Hamilton Cheevers looked like he was born to wear one. The tailored cut of the jacket emphasized his wide shoulders. He removed the jacket to reveal firm, muscular arms and a crisply creased white button-down Oxford shirt. Bettina admired the way his body tapered down to a trim waist and hips. She imagined he must work out. Many men his age had let themselves go, but not the editor. It was clear he took rigorous care of himself. Her eyes strayed to the thick black leather belt around his waist. She closed her eyes briefly as the thought of that belt striping her bottom with red passed through her lust-filled mind. She gulped and felt her cheeks turn pink.

"Shall we sit down, Tina?" the editor said with a slight smirk on his face, as if he could read her mind. Tina nodded, her legs trembling.

He held the chair for her and she sat, impressed by his impeccable manners. It had been years since any man had shown her such respect.

They chatted about everything while they ate, and then they discussed her story.

"I was impressed with how well you described your character's desire to submit. Have you always known you were submissive?"

"No. I didn't know at all. But I do now. She is me. I didn't really understand that until I wrote this story."

"A most astute realization." He smiled and reached again for her hand. His touch turned her skin to fire.

"You made me realize it, didn't you? You guided me toward this right from the start. But you didn't tell me. Why?"

"You needed to come to your own realization. My role is to guide, not to force."

"Thank you, Sir. I would like to show you my gratitude."

"Yes, Tina, and you will. Let's walk off this food."

He rose and moved to her, raising her up and letting his hand linger on the small of her back.

"Oh," she sighed.

"Is something the matter?"

"No, Sir, not at all. The opposite, in fact. This feels so right. Your hands on me."

"Yes. I know. It feels right to have you under my hand, Tina."

They walked out into the late spring air and watched a fireworks display. The streets were empty all around them. He took her hand and pulled her into a dark alley.

"Kneel, Tina. I need your mouth around my cock." He spread his coat on the sidewalk.

Bettina paused. *What if someone sees?* she thought. She

looked into his eyes, dark with desire. She wanted to please him, but she was torn. Her body ached to obey, yet she worried about being caught.

"I won't let anything happen to you." He stroked her hair, running his fingers along her back. Then he touched her collar again. "You're mine." His voice was commanding and certain. The feel of his hands at her neck drove away her uncertainty. Yes, she was his, his slave. At that moment she knew she'd do anything for him, anything to please him.

"Show me, Tina. Prove you're mine." His fingers traced her collar, then glided underneath her dress, finding her nipples, stroking them stiff.

Her body hummed. Her nipples felt singed by his touch, his ownership of her.

"Yes, Sir," Tina said, her voice taking on a raspy, parched tone as she moved to the ground. Her master held her head firmly as she unzipped him, and he placed his fingers on the back of her neck, caressing her collar.

She took out his cock, which was hard and uncut. Wrapping her hands around his shaft, she uncovered the glans. Tina breathed hotly against him and took the head in her mouth, opening wide to accommodate its thick girth. She'd done this before, but never really enjoyed it. Now she needed it. Needed to swallow him. He stayed still while she licked around his cock and encircled his shaft with firm fingers.

"Yes, girl. Take it," he said as he grabbed the back of her head and forced her forward so that his cock pressed deeply down her throat.

"Now look up at me."

She looked up then, lapping at his cock with her tongue. She felt the head of his cock pulsing as it moved in and out of her mouth.

"Lick the rim," he said.

She circled the edge of the head with her tongue, feeling his balls tighten against her chin.

"Now take my come. Drink it."

Short bursts of salty come spurted out of the slit of his cock-head and down Bettina's throat. She drank it all down. Her master's come filled her, quenched her. Her cunt tingled and her breasts heaved as he kept coming.

Afterward he lifted her up from her knees and held her tightly to him, raising her dress.

"You're soaking, Tina. You want this. You want me to use you, don't you?"

"Yes, Sir. Yes, please."

Her legs trembled as he pressed his fingers inside her cunt.

"Lean against me then. I want to feel your juices flow for me."

She humped her cunt onto his hot, cupped hand. He braced her against him, wrapping his arms around her back, and pulled her toward him. His fingers were warm inside her.

"Open for me now. Take me in."

She took a sharp breath and allowed herself to let go. She wanted his cock, needed it so badly, she found herself begging to be taken.

"Please, your cock. I want it."

She felt the sting of his other hand against her buttocks.

"I'll give you my cock when you've come for me. Move."

Her breath ragged, she stopped thinking and let herself be mastered. She'd never done this outside before. Never trusted anyone else to do this to her. She spread herself wider and clenched, letting his hand move deeper into her soaking cunt. She moved her hips back and forth against his fingers—her master's fingers—so deep, so strong. She felt the pulsing of her orgasm start to churn against her clit and inside her cunt as he curled his fingers upward, beckoning her to come.

She was a flame shivering in the darkness against him, burning them both with need as she clutched at his fingers with her cunt.

He brought her chin up with his other hand and forced his tongue deeply into her mouth, licking at her tongue, sucking it, biting her lips as she trembled and humped quicker against his hand.

"Ask my permission," he whispered. "Ask me to let you come."

Those words put her over the edge.

"Please, I need…may…may I come?"

"Yes! Come for me, my Tina. Come. Now."

She let go then. Came for him. Juices flowed all over his hand. The musky scent of their sex combined with the odor of smoke in the air.

He brought his fingers up to her lips.

"Open your mouth."

She had never tasted herself before. She had always been disgusted by the idea, but for him, she opened. She trusted him.

The sharp, sweet taste filled her mouth. She cried out as she licked every drop of the evidence of her surrender from his hand. Her tongue tasted each fingertip, slid down in between each finger, traced the lines in his palm. He rubbed his hand over her face, down inside her dress, reaching in to twist her nipples. They were hard and ready for his touch.

"I always want these nipples hard and your cunt wet. Do you understand, Tina?"

"Yes, Sir."

"When you come to me or I come to you, you will always be ready to serve me."

Bettina looked into his eyes. She had no doubts, no uncertainty. This was what she wanted, this was who she was.

"Open for me, Tina. Belong to me. I promise you fire." He kissed her again then, a long kiss that burned against her lips. She opened her mouth and accepted his tongue and his promise as he mastered her. Completely.

RIBBONS

Kathryn O'Halloran

Lilly receives the box in the mail. She opens it carefully. She hasn't heard from him for two weeks and she wonders if she's ruined things. As she runs her nail under a line of sticky tape, she smiles. Surely this is a peace offering wrapped in a command. She removes the lid and her smile curdles. She doesn't understand. Coiled amongst the black, crumpled tissue paper are three ribbons, jewel toned and velvet. One purple, one green, one red.

She reads the note beneath and drops the box onto the floor.

They met when she wandered, brain-addled, into a nearby bar. Returning from a holiday that delivered little, she muddled in that halfway state—not home, yet not somewhere else. She never went to bars alone. Not ever. But her apartment had lost her smell and her head buzzed, soft and low, like the bass line from a song she'd heard once a long time ago.

The bar was nothing special, a jumble of mismatched furniture and florid paintings, eclectic style, the shiniest of people in low-cut jeans waving their arms in the air to music a couple of notches louder than comfortable. Lilly sat on a bar stool with a ripped vinyl seat. No matter how she moved, the edge dug into her thigh. She tried to cross her legs but her muscles were unyielding.

The music dulled the buzzing in her head; the whiskey stopped her caring about it. She tore at a napkin, wondering if she'd drunk enough to sleep.

She caught him looking—not at her directly but at her reflection in the mirror behind the bar. A fractured her, broken up by glasses and bottles. She didn't know what he saw; she didn't even think she'd be able to pick herself out of a crowd. Her face looked faded, like a rag doll left in the sun.

He looked unshaven and unkempt. Dirty, lean and sly. His fingers circled his glass like spiders. He repulsed her, causing a lurch in her guts.

As she turned away, the jagged vinyl scratched her legs. She felt her thigh redden. But she wouldn't look. She tucked her skirt in around her thighs, hoping to protect them, and stared into the distance, but her movements were self-conscious at the possibility that he could be watching. She wouldn't turn and give him the satisfaction. She'd been walled inside herself for years. She hadn't come out looking for this. She hadn't come out looking for anything.

Yet, despite herself, she turned briefly to glimpse his hands, the knuckles too large for the fingers, the nails ragged and dirty.

The buzzing inside her grew louder, louder than the music, louder than the traffic outside, louder than the whole world. She'd never sleep now. She'd walk. Walk and walk and walk until she dropped from exhaustion. Maybe then her mind would be still. She stood up and wrapped herself tightly into her coat but even that didn't stop the shivers.

As he followed her out, she felt in her pocket for her keys. If he came too close, she'd jam them in his eye socket. But he come close and she didn't resist. His fingers brushed lightly on her sleeve, nothing more than that. It felt right, like he'd drawn her in from a ledge on a tall, tall building where she'd swayed in the wind. He warmed her and numbed her and gave her peace.

She stares at the ribbons, snaking across the floor. The colors glow against the dark floorboards—amethyst and emerald and ruby. He's asked her to pick one and wear it tonight. This wasn't part of the bargain. Lilly is the girl who can't make up her mind. Lilly is the girl who acquiesces. Lilly wants oblivion. But *he* wants her to be present.

She nudges at the ribbons with her toe as though they are living creatures liable to rear up and attack if she isn't vigilant.

She might freeze before she works them out. She might freeze here like a statue. Before that can happen, she puts on her coat and thrusts the ribbons in her pocket. She'll destroy them. She'll walk to the river and throw them in. They'll sink deep down where no one will ever see them.

"Fuck you," she says, quietly and under her breath. She'll throw the ribbons and keep moving, until she finds someone who demands nothing from her.

She walks with her arms folded, hands deep into her armpits. The woollen edges of her coat prickle her throat and her breath rises in steamy clouds around her. She walks with a singular stride, bowling through anyone who gets in her way. If she keeps walking, she won't feel cold; she won't freeze like a statue. She won't hear this buzzing. At the lights, she hammers her thumb against the button over and over, anxious to keep moving. Block after block of squealing schoolkids and mothers with prams and beggars wanting change. She leaves them all behind.

He never fucks her. The first few times, he barely touches her. He takes her to a near-empty room, like an abandoned garage with a sink and a hot plate and the lingering smell of petroleum, a concrete floor and barely lined walls, but still she doesn't feel cold.

An old wooden chair sits in the middle of the room—a throne, and she is going to be a queen.

He orders her to remove her clothes but turns from her while she undresses. As he ties her to the chair, the precision of the knots surprises her. The exactness belies his crumbled appearance. She pulls against the ropes, trying to free herself, pulls until they burn red into her skin, but is glad they hold firm. The buzzing in her mind stills.

He wraps a cloth around her eyes with expertise, blocking out the light. No red flashes or pinpoints of color, just total true black. Her breathing slows, coming from the depths of her belly.

His hands hover near her, radiating warmth, but they don't make contact with her skin. She can smell him, earthy and sour; she can hear the faint shuffle of his steps, but these things are outside her. And even though he doesn't touch her, even though she doesn't come, her body slumps in a postorgasmic surrender.

When he finally releases her, she lies inert, as though her skeleton has softened. The ropes still dangle from her wrists but she can't move. She's a marionette with no one to work her strings. The outside world seems harsh and bright and abrasive.

The next time she sees him, she's all sinew and tendons. She begs him to take it away, to give her peace. He tethers her and strokes her clean.

The colors could mean anything. Red is fire and passion and danger. Green is nature and growth and jealously. Purple is royal.

But she can't think how he'd mean any of that. Red means stop and green means go, which leaves purple meaning nothing.

She pulls the purple ribbon out of her pocket and twists the fuzzy edge around her fingers. The velvet is soft and fine and yielding.

One time when she was leaving, he handed her a purple flower and told her to wear it in her hair so he'd be able to pick her out in a crowd. It startled her to think he saw her at times outside his room. After that, she looked for him at the train station and in the lunchtime crush but she never saw him. Still, she imagined him watching over her and she felt safe. She wore the flower until it wilted and turned brown.

She takes out the green ribbon, twisting it around the purple.

When they are together, after he's done, he brings her tea in a green mug. It's chipped and she pretends she doesn't see the stains inside. She doesn't like tea but she needs something to bridge the gap between him and the rest of her life. While she sips the tea, she readjusts. The tea is strong and sweet and milky. Workman's tea. And even though she doesn't like it, she drinks it when he gives it to her, her hands wrapped around the scalding, green mug. Sips it and fills herself with its robustness. It's the green he wants her to pick.

She takes out the red ribbon and weaves it through the other two as if making some complicated cat's cradle.

Red is the color of her blindfold, the screen he brings between her and the rest of the world. Soft yet strong. He treasures the cloth, folds it gently and returns it to a special box while everything around him is covered in a layer of dust. When he takes the cloth in his hands, she knows he delights in its feel. He runs it though his fingers and sometimes even smiles. Five times he's smiled. Barely noticeable, just a twitch at the corner of his mouth and a crinkle at the corner of his eyes but a smile nonetheless and then his voice becomes thick like syrup. It's the red he means.

The ribbons tangle around her fingers until she wonders if she'll be able to separate them.

It's a test, but she doesn't think it's a test she'll pass. The note said to trust him, to trust herself and she'll know. But she doesn't know, so already she's failed. Why does he leave her to guess? He's supposed to be the one taking *her* hand, the one pulling *her* in from the ledge, but it feels like his hands aren't guiding her in, they're behind her, pushing her. She's falling.

When she gets to the river, she climbs onto the bridge. She holds the ribbons up high against the dull, gray sky. They look so pretty.

Boats float in random patterns below her. They rock with the flow of the water. She leans her head against the metal rail, watching. They are anchored like she is not. She's a boat and she's adrift. He's a landmass.

Lately he's wanted more. He wants her to react. He shackles her but stares at her for a long time before he covers her eyes, cupping her face in his hands so that the impression lasts long after he's gone. He pets her slow and soft like she's a rare breed of cat. Other times he ignores her, leaving her alone and unguarded. He talks to her—sometimes in a language she can't understand, more often asking questions she can't answer. He touches her softly, trailing the rough pad of his finger over her neck and her breasts and her legs. His touch becomes firmer, squeezing and kneading and pummeling. He commands her into various positions so that he can probe and explore every part of her.

But from the moment he ties her, she's gone. No pleasure, no pain, just emptiness.

He sighs as he unties her.

She looks up, stunned at his defeat. "Tell me, and I'll do it."
But he shakes his head.

She promises to do anything he asks. He turns away like
she isn't there and spoons tea into a pot, trailing an unraveling
sleeve. She waits for a response. When he turns back to her, he
stares at her for a long time. Then he asks her if she's prepared
to give up the surrender.

She frowns. She can't separate the act from the man.

She hears nothing more, not until the ribbons.

She leans on the railings, holding out her hand. The ribbons
stream out from her fingers, dangling in the wind. She thinks
she's ready to let go when someone pulls her back. Arms around
her, pulling her down, so rough they bruise her skin. A stranger
with the authority of his assumptions.

"What the fuck do you think you're doing?" he shouts into
her face. Her rescuer is big and burly, wrapped in a padded
jacket. He's not the rescuer she wants.

She hunches down and laughs. She's not a jumper. She holds
out the ribbons.

"Which one would you pick?" she asks.

He shakes his head and walks back to his truck, getting out
a phone. As he starts punching in the numbers, she stands and
walks away.

"Come back, you crazy bitch," the stranger screams but she
keeps on walking.

That night he meets her at the door. Her face is grimy and
streaked with tears. Her fingers are stiff with cold.

She holds out the red ribbon and he smiles.

"It's the right one?" she asks. She doesn't look up. She can't
read his face and the buzzing deafens her mind.

He pulls the ribbon through her fingers.

"There was no right one."

As the soft leather of his gloved fingers circles her wrist, her pulse pounds beneath his touch. She feels alive.

THE DAY I CAME IN PUBLIC

D. L. King

L isten honey," Marla said, "don't knock it until you've tried it."

At the time, the idea of calling your boyfriend "Sir" and letting him order you around didn't strike me as the sexy romance she made it out to be. "Are you telling me he hits you?" I grabbed her hand across the table. "Marla! Do you have bruises? Has he hurt you?"

"Listen, it's not like that. It isn't abuse," she said. I let her hand go but continued to stare at her over my martini. "Don't jump to conclusions. I want you to make me a promise. I'm gonna give you a book to read. Read it and then we'll talk again. Promise me you'll keep an open mind until then."

She reached into her workbag and pulled out a well-worn paperback. "What is this? Porn?" I asked. "What, you just carry this stuff around with you all the time now? I don't know what's happening to you, Marla. I'm afraid for you."

"I figured you'd be a hard sell and I wanted to be prepared. Just read it, Libby, then we'll talk."

I looked down at the book on the table. It was the first volume in that fairy-tale trilogy. I'd heard about it but hadn't read it. "I don't know what difference you think it'll make, my reading a fairy tale. I'm worried about you," I repeated.

"Read the book. We'll meet here next Friday after work, and we can talk more then. I don't want to discuss it anymore, not 'til you've read the book."

"But Marla..."

"Nope! What I want to talk about now is Joe and Holly. I walked in on them in the copy room yesterday. I gotta go to the bathroom. Order me another drink, will you? I'll be right back."

I was a little concerned, but she seemed fine and when she returned from the ladies' room we got off on another topic. Between the vodka and a long workweek, I couldn't concentrate on anything heavy anyway. I forgot all about Marla's crazy boyfriend and the book until Saturday afternoon, when I remembered I hadn't taken care of my empty lunch container from Friday. I took the Tupperware out of my bag and noticed the book hiding underneath.

I took it out. Pretty cover. I didn't recognize the author's name. I seemed to recall this was written by someone famous, but under an assumed name. It must be pretty dirty for the writer not to want to own up to it. Why the hell would he—she, whatever—want to hide unless they were ashamed? But I remembered hearing that lots of writers, famous ones, published their books under false names, pseudonyms, like Mark Twain. I didn't have time for this anyway. I had laundry and housecleaning to do. I left the book on the coffee table and promptly forgot about it.

When I finally settled down to relax in front of the TV, there was nothing on. I thought about watching a DVD but couldn't get excited about anything in my collection. That's when I noticed the book.

Three hours later, a little out of breath and with drenched underwear shoved tightly between the swollen lips of my pussy, I realized it was after midnight. Holy fuck! I needed to go to bed—but first I needed to find my vibrator.

The end of the week finally came and Marla and I left work at five on the dot to secure a table at our favorite haunt.

"Well?" she said.

"Yeah, okay."

"Yeah, okay, what?"

"Yeah, okay, I get it."

"And?" She grinned.

"Yeah, yeah, okay, it was hot," I conceded.

"Can I pick 'em or can I pick 'em?" she asked the ether. Directing her attention to me once more, she said, "I just knew if you understood, you'd get it and be turned on. So?"

"So, what? That stuff isn't real. I mean it's hot but those things don't happen. No place like that really exists and no one does those kinds of things really. I mean, it's a hot fantasy, but that's all it is."

"Of course that's a fantasy. But you'd be surprised what there really is, what people get up to, what's out there if you look for it. I know you want to know more." And then she proceeded to give me a primer in kinky sex and how to find it.

Once I started looking, I couldn't believe how much there was. All of a sudden I understood the true purpose of the Internet. I researched and researched and couldn't believe what I'd been missing all my life. Who knew? Well, I guess everyone but me. Sometimes I'm slow on the uptake.

I joined lists. I joined chats. I read lots of smut. I watched lots and lots of porn. Finally, I took an online friend up on attending a public meeting at a local diner. I liked him. He was obviously intelligent and seemed to know what he was talking about. He also made me cream my jeans every time I saw his name in my inbox.

He was the domliest of doms. We'd be chatting about art or work or something equally innocuous and he'd write something like, *Pull your pants down to your ankles. Pull your panties down to the top of your pants. Now, sit back down. No touching,* then he'd continue on with whatever we'd been chatting about before.

Just when all the wet was beginning to dry up, he'd refocus my attention to my bare ass and naked pussy. He seemed to know just when to give me another sexual push to keep me on edge. Sometimes at the end of our correspondence for the evening, he'd take pity on me and give me permission to come but, as often as not, he'd tell me to go straight to bed—if I couldn't keep my hands off myself, he'd dictate, I was only permitted to touch my nipples. Yeah, that would make for some seriously sleepless nights.

I'd find myself thinking of him at odd times. In the middle of my commute to work, his last email would pop into my head and completely carry me away from reality. I'd be sure the people on the bus could smell me. Or worse, I'd be in a sales meeting and the same thing would happen. I'd have to fight to keep focused. So of course the idea of finally meeting him in the flesh, as it were, was exciting, and a little scary.

It was scary because I didn't know how I'd act around him. I had my idea of what he looked like, but what if I was wrong? All I knew for sure was that he had dark hair and was physically fit. What if I wasn't attracted to him? What if I was? God, what if he wasn't attracted to me? Scary.

I was definitely attracted to the personality I knew online. He was my ideal, I suppose. He wasn't the "On your knees, slave, lick my balls," kind of dom. I'd met plenty of them online and I couldn't take those guys seriously. I mean, really! No, he was someone who wanted the same things I wanted, someone I could believe in, someone I could take seriously because he took both me, and himself, seriously. I could tell this guy wasn't playing, even when he was playing.

"Libby?"

I must have looked totally lost. I'm not all that outgoing under normal circumstances, but here I was, standing by the door of the back room of a diner, looking at ten or fifteen total strangers, all of whom were into kinky sex to one degree or another. A woman was making her way toward me with a welcoming look just as I heard the masculine voice behind me.

"Libby?" I turned and he smiled. "Hi. I'm Chris. I'm glad you made it."

My mind was on autopilot as he introduced me to all the people. All these thoughts swam through my consciousness: *Chris. Wow, he's short. Great voice. Gee, I didn't know he wore glasses. Nice ass; yeah, he is pretty fit. Look at those eyes. That voice, God, that voice. He's hot—I think he's hot—he's...look at those hands. He's talking about buffalo wings and I'm getting wet....*

Finally, things started wrapping up and people began to leave. "Shall we go somewhere and chat?" he suggested.

We went to a quiet pub and talked until they closed, then made plans to meet at the diner the following Saturday. We'd go to a private S/M club so that I could watch people play—watch him play. He wanted to take things slowly.

The week seemed to crawl by. I met Marla at the bar on

Friday, as usual, and she asked how the meeting went. I told her all about it and about how I was going to the Mansion on Saturday.

"Ooh, I love that place. Hey, maybe I'll see you there. Are you going to play?"

"In public? I don't think so! I could never get naked in public—um, do people really get naked there?"

"Sure. Sometimes. Sometimes they leave on some stuff. It depends. But if you aren't going to play, why are you going?"

"Chris wants me to watch. He said it would be good for me to see what it's like, to watch the doms and see the reactions of the people on the receiving end. He said he wanted me to watch him play with someone before I made a decision about allowing him to play with me. He wants to make sure I'm comfortable with everything. He doesn't like to jump into things."

An email was waiting for me when I got home.

> *We'll meet at the diner at 8:00 tomorrow evening. From there I will escort you to the Mansion. Wear a skirt, something short and flouncy, not black. Wear a feminine blouse that buttons in the front. If you feel you must wear stockings, no panty hose. You may either wear thigh-high stockings or stockings with a garter belt. I'll leave the choice of shoes up to you, however my preference would be heels that lengthen your legs and show off your calves. Oh yes, no panties or bra.*
>
> *Chris*

I had to go shopping. I didn't own most of that stuff. I seldom wore skirts, and when I did, they were only slightly above the knee, and straight. Most of my clothes were black, or at least dark. I'm a New Yorker, after all! I needed to buy stockings. I decided to go for thigh-high stay-ups rather than a garter belt. A garter belt sounded really hot, but it also sounded like a lot of trouble, especially if this never happened again. I had a closet full of shoes; they were the one thing I wouldn't have to buy for this date. Was this a date?

I became more and more nervous, preparing for my evening with Chris. I wondered about everything. Would he like the smell of my soap and shampoo? Should I wear perfume, and if so, what fragrance would he prefer? I worried about my hair; should I wear it up or down? Should I try to curl it or leave it straight? Everything had to be just right.

I worried he wouldn't like the outfit I'd chosen, a ruffled miniskirt with little flowers on a blue background. I'd bought a darker blue silk blouse to go with it. While I might never wear the skirt again, at least the blouse would be a keeper. I decided on platinum strappy sandals with a four-inch spiked heel and hoped I wouldn't have to do much walking.

As I fussed with my makeup, I became more aware of the missing panties. It was an odd sensation. Depending on how careful I was when I sat, I often found my bare bottom making contact with the chair. At least the fullness of the skirt draped well over my thighs, and with my legs together no one would be able to see my pussy. As that thought entered my consciousness, I felt the first hints of moisture. This could be bad! Just before leaving, I put on the stockings and shoes. Somehow, the stay-up stockings made me feel even more naked than I had before. The silicone material at the tops, which caused them to stay up without garters, hugged my thighs and made me even more conscious of my bareness.

I arrived at the diner fifteen minutes early and waited outside for Chris. As I saw him round the corner at precisely 8:00, my heart sped. He wore black leather pants, which fit him perfectly, not too loose and not too tight; a charcoal, long-sleeved shirt and black leather boots. Somehow, he no longer looked short; in fact, he looked rather imposing. I hadn't noticed how sexy his Hugh Grant hair was before, and his glasses somehow added to his air of control.

"You look lovely," he said, ushering me into the restaurant.

"So do you," I murmured.

Over salads and sandwiches he talked about the club and answered my questions. "Even though you won't be playing tonight, I want you to do exactly as I say. Afterward, with your permission, I'll take you home and we'll chat about your experiences and feelings. I like your choice of outfits," he said. I felt his hand on my leg, stroking me through my stockings. He moved it up to the stocking top and ran his finger along the edge briefly. My breath caught as his fingers worked their way past the stocking top and up to the fold of my thigh. He slowly shifted direction until his hand cupped my uncovered sex. "Good girl," he said, taking his hand away. He picked up his napkin and blotted his mouth. "Shall we?"

Silk may not have been the best choice for my blouse. My nipples felt like they would poke straight through the material, and his brushing the back of his hand against one while we stood at the cash register didn't help. Outside again, he hailed a cab and I scooted into the back and did my best to sit on my skirt, squeezing my legs closed.

As it was still early, there weren't many patrons at the Mansion when we arrived. Most people seemed to know him and they said hello. He chatted with a few, who either smiled at me or scrutinized me. Not once did he introduce me or mention me, but he kept his hand on the small of my back the whole time.

Using his hand, as if we were dancing, he directed me through the entire club, showing me all the different rooms, explaining what each was for and drawing my attention to different pieces of equipment and furniture. I was sure juices were dripping down my legs by the time the tour was over. We moved to the bar and he ordered me a bottle of water. "Wait here for a minute. Don't talk to anyone. I'll be right back."

One guy in jeans and a black leather vest blatantly stared at me but didn't come over. A woman in a tight black rubber dress smiled and made her way to the bar. "Hi lovey," she said. "Is this your first time here? My name's Hennie, short for Henrietta. You're a sweet little thing. I'm sure I would have remembered if I'd seen you before." As she reached over, Chris returned.

"Hi Hennie, she's with me."

"Sure Chris, no problem. Anyway honey, you get tired of this guy, you just remember Hennie."

Chris brought me to another room, with a raised platform and benches lining the walls. He led me to a bench directly across from a man and woman. "George has graciously given me permission to play with his girl. You sit here," he said. "You'll get the best view and I'll be able to watch you as well. George'll be watching, and other people may come in to watch, too, you never know." He sat me down in the middle of the bench, which was only about ten feet from the stage. "I'll play with Becca for about an hour, and then we'll leave."

I straightened my skirt over my thighs and made sure my legs were together. The bench was low, so with my heels on, my knees were higher than my thighs. I took great pains to keep them glued to each other so I wouldn't be exposed.

"One last thing," Chris said. "Stand up." He lifted the back of my skirt and had me place my bare bottom on the bench. "I want you to keep your legs open the entire time you're watching." He put his hands on my knees and moved my legs about a foot apart, putting me on display for George or anyone else who happened to look.

"But Chris, I…"

He put a finger to my lips. "Remember our agreement? No one will bother you; they all know you're with me. Would you rather I took you home instead?"

I felt on the edge of tears. "No, Chris."

"Good girl. The room lights will be turned down and there will be spotlights on the stage. No one will see you, or even know to look, but me. Now remember, even if you get excited and want to squeeze your legs together, don't. We'll each be able to gauge your reaction better this way. Don't move until I come for you. Clear?"

"Yes, Chris." I couldn't believe I was acting like this, but I simply couldn't react any other way. It was as if I had no choice and had lost the willpower to do anything other than what Chris wished. It was both scary and hot and I felt wetness seeping out of me. God, but I wanted to squeeze my legs closed.

The room lights went down, the stage lights came up and Becca appeared. He had her take off her clothes and then he fastened her wrists to chains attached to the ceiling, suspending them above shoulder level. He put cuffs on her ankles and had her spread her legs. There were eyebolts in the floor to which he fastened her ankle cuffs.

He started by stroking her body: long, gentle strokes with his hands. I couldn't believe she could be there, so naked and open, in public like that, but as she began to react to his touch, that thought went out of my mind and I could only think of the sensations she must be feeling—and the sensations I was feeling.

Chris began squeezing her breasts, gently at first, but then harder, until she cried out. He squeezed and pulled her nipples, elongating them, and then attached clamps to them. It looked painful and I saw her wince. He attached weights to the clamps. They were heavy enough to pull her nipples downward. He brushed his hands against the weights, setting them swinging. I could see her nipples being pulled from side to side by the clamps as the weights swung. Her breasts were large, larger than mine. I wondered what that would feel like. My nipples weren't overly sensitive, but they *were* sensitive.

As I mused about my nipples, Chris added the same type of clamp and weight arrangement to her pussy lips, but this time the weights looked heavier, stretching them far from her opening. By now, a constant trickle of moisture had begun to leak from my open pussy. It tickled and itched and fought for my attention.

Chris attached a delicate clip, with a bell on the end, to Becca's clit. It looked something like a bobby pin. He played with the bell on the end, making it ring. With each flick of his fingers, the girl moaned and I gushed. My God, I felt like I was sitting in a puddle.

Next, he moved behind her and used a thin cane on her bottom. He seemed to strike her lightly, almost gently, but she winced or moaned with each strike. It made me wonder what that would feel like on *my* bum. After a while, the bell began to ring and he stopped. He gently stroked her ass, where the cane had just fallen, and whispered something to her. She sighed and closed her eyes and I imagined being in her place and must have closed my eyes, too.

I heard a smack and my eyes flew open. He stood in front of her again, this time with a riding crop. She hung from her chains, leaning slightly forward. Chris used the crop to smack the sides of each breast, causing the weights to swing in ever-widening arcs, until she released tiny, high-pitched screams. At that point, he used his hands to steady the weights and whispered to her again.

He used the flat of the crop against her shaved mound, just above where the clip hung. I hadn't noticed until then that she was shaved. I think her smooth, hairless flesh made the smack from the crop sound louder than it would have otherwise. All I know is that shortly after he began hitting her there, the bell began to ring intermittently, until, after a while, its clear tone rang out continuously. He continued until her hips began to thrash back and forth.

He put down the crop and cupped the weights and clamps in his hand, and gently removed them, first from one lip, then from the other. Leaving the clit clip on, he gently massaged the area while he spoke to her. When she nodded her head, he stopped the massage and slowly removed the weights from her nipple clamps. With the removal of each weight, her clit bell jingled. My clit felt like it was three times its normal size.

He whispered something else and she shook her head no. He spoke to her again, and again she shook her head. Using his bare hand, he spanked her ass. Based on the sound his hand made, I'd guess it was pretty hard. Again, he spoke to her and this time she nodded in the affirmative. He gently removed the clamps from her nipples and she screamed. Quickly, he used his hands to massage them and then he used his mouth on them.

When he took his hands away, I could see the deep impressions the clamps had left in her skin and how red her nipples were. More liquid gushed from my sopping cunt. He removed the clit bell and unfastened her ankles. He helped her bring her feet to a more normal stance and George came over to hold her while Chris undid her wrist cuffs.

As the room lights came up, I looked around. Somehow, without my noticing, the room had filled with people. They slowly got up and began to file out as Chris came over to me. He put a box down on the bench, leaned down and put his hands on my knees.

"I see you were not unaffected by the performance," he said, looking at the puddle of wet I was sitting in. All I could do was moan.

"Lean your head against my chest," he whispered, "and grind that nasty fuckin' cunt into the bench. Do it now. There's no way you'll be able to walk out of here otherwise."

God help me, I did it. I shoved my naked wet cunt against a hard bench in a room with strangers walking in and out. I rocked against that bench until I shook with release, and what was possibly the most intense sexual itch I'd ever had began to subside. Chris handed me the box of wet wipes. I looked up at him.

"Clean the bench, too. Then I'll take you home. It's still early, you know."

LUNCH

Elizabeth Coldwell

It's five to twelve, and I am waiting for his email. Like every other day, it will come on the dot of midday, and like every other day, it will tell me what I can have for lunch and where I can eat it. If I have been good—and I always think I have, because I try so hard to live up to the standards Michael sets for me—I might be allowed to go and sit in the sandwich bar across the road with Jo and Carly and have a mochaccino and a slice of carrot cake with cream cheese icing. If I have been bad, then I will have to sit on my own in my office, picking at a boring green salad. It's a ritual that has existed between us for almost a year now, and it has come to define the way our relationship has developed since the moment I first realized I like it when he takes control.

I've never explained to anyone why my eating arrangements vary so much from day to day. Mention that my husband is telling me what to do, and people will be expecting me to walk in one morning with bruises on my face and the excuse that I walked into a door. Say that it's a domination game and they'll peg us as a couple of sickos into whips and chains and all manner of unspeakable acts. So I make some comment about work piling up and not having the time to leave my desk, or let everyone think I'm on the latest diet from the pages of a glossy magazine. After all, how many of the women here don't have some strange, self-inflicted restrictions on what they eat, whether that's cutting out meat and dairy, passing on the carbs, or existing on nothing but coffee, cigarettes and fresh air?

Still, I shouldn't have to worry about any of that today—or so I think. And then the mail icon is bouncing insistently at the bottom of my screen, and I know his instructions have arrived. I click on the message and scan his words. *Sorry, no date with the girls today. If you'd wanted a treat, you should have remembered to pick up my gray suit from the dry cleaner's.* Guiltily, I slide open the top drawer of my desk. There, tucked into the pages of my diary, is the green receipt from the dry cleaning concession in the tube station precinct. The receipt for the suit I should have collected on the way home from work last night. I carry on reading. *Lunch will be ham and salad on granary bread, mayonnaise but no butter, and a bottle of orange juice. You will also buy a banana, the greenest and most unripe in the sandwich bar. You will not eat the banana. Instead, you will use it to pleasure yourself at your desk, and you will think of me while you do so.*

I read the last couple of sentences again. This is something new. Something dangerous. It wouldn't be the first time I've played with myself at work. In the early days of our relationship, before I had ever begun to explore the submissive side of my personality, Michael used to send me emails describing what he was going to do to me when I got home, emails so filthy and explicit I would rush off to the ladies' and bring myself to a swift, sharp climax, muffling my moans by jamming the fleshy part of my thumb into my mouth. But in the relative open of my office, where someone could walk in and catch me at it? Of course, I could go home and just tell Michael I'd done as he instructed. But he would know. He always knows when I try to disobey him, however careful or sneaky I try to be. And besides, the thought excites me just as much as it alarms me. It must do: otherwise why would my pussy be pulsing quite so hard against the silky crotch of my underwear?

Time drags for the next hour. It's almost impossible to concentrate on my work; all I can think of are Michael's instructions, but then I'm sure he intended it that way. Finally, it's one o'clock, and I log off my workstation, grab my handbag and go out to get my lunch.

It's unseasonably warm, and people have left their coats and jackets indoors and are basking in the spring sunshine. As I wait to cross the road, I find myself, as always, watching the women who pass by, checking them out to see if they bear some subtle mark of ownership. I can spot the signs by now: the discreet tattoo on the ankle or shoulder blade; the black velvet choker or thick silver band around the neck that is rather more than just a fashionable piece of jewelry.

There are scenes being played out all around us every day, as seemingly mundane yet undeniably kinky as the one between Michael and me. Sometimes, you can walk into one without even realizing it. We were shopping in town the other week, and he came in the changing rooms with me as I went to try on a dress. As we made our way down the row of cubicles to find one that was vacant, a curtain was suddenly whisked aside by the man who stood outside it. He made some casual enquiry to his wife about the bathing suit she was squeezing into, as though he hadn't noticed we were there, and all the time he was giving us a perfect view of her body, tits and pussy blatantly on display and the sky blue fabric of the swimsuit bunched around her knees. Her face was blushing red, and yet I saw in her eyes the thrill she was getting from her exposure and humiliation. This was what got the two of them off, and I was sure that when Michael and I had gone, he would pin her up against the cubicle partition and fuck her to a standstill as they teased each other about what they had just done.

It worked for them, just as my lunchtime ritual works for me, this setting of a so-simple rule that marks the level of trust between Michael and me.

For once there's no queue in the sandwich bar, and I give my order to the young man behind the counter, one of the extended family of Turks who own the place. He's chatty as always, but I'm not listening to a word he's saying, just nodding when he holds up the pepper mill, muttering a token word of thanks as he hands the sandwich, wrapped in a paper bag, to me. All I'm thinking about is the fruit bowl next to the till, and the slender, underripe banana I reach out and take from it. As I hand over my money to the girl behind the till, I think I see her glance at the banana and smile. Does she realize what I'm going to do with it? Is it really as obvious to everyone as I feel it must be? My cheeks flush scarlet, and then she says something in Turkish and I realize she's responding to some conversation in the kitchen, nothing to do with me at all. Chastened, I pocket my change without checking it and make my way back to the office on autopilot, the last ordinary act of this extraordinary lunch hour.

I don't even unwrap the sandwich; I have no appetite for food, just a nervous fluttering in my stomach and an answering pulse between my legs. The door to my office doesn't lock, so I jam the wastepaper basket up against it. Anyone tries to come in and I'll hear the rattle and stop what I'm doing—assuming I'm not too far gone to stop, that is.

Quickly, inelegantly, I reach up under my skirt and yank down my knickers. I haven't even touched myself yet and they are already sticky with my juice. Michael's orders and my own imagination have got me this excited, and I only wish he was here to watch me.

Making myself as comfortable as I can in my chair, I push my skirt up and spread my legs. I can feel the fabric of the seat cover, rough and prickly against my bare arse. I'm trying to remember every sensation, every detail, because I suspect that when I get home, I will be asked to describe it to my husband, reliving every deliciously dirty moment of what I'm about to do.

The banana is firm in my hand, and feels cool to the touch as I run the blunt head along the length of my sex. If Michael were here, he would want me to take my time, make sure I'm wet and open enough to take this unorthodox toy, just as he likes it when I spend long, lazy moments fingering my clit and gently teasing my hole, getting it ready for my favorite dildo or the hot length of his cock. But time is the one thing I don't have, not when the boys in the advertising department could be back, loud and boisterous, from their liquid lunch at any moment. If this was a fantasy that I was spinning for Michael, of course, they would blunder in and catch me, force me to continue as I tried to cover myself up, make me bare my tits for them, maybe even queue up to fuck me in turn over the desk, ramming their cocks into my pussy as the flesh of the banana oozed out around their thrusts. But this is real life—however skewed—and all I have are my own busily working fingers to stroke me and stretch me open.

It doesn't take long before I know I'm ready to be filled. Eyes closed, breathing hard, I press the banana home, feeling the strange, hard ridges sliding against my soft flesh. I know this is the most perverse, most risky, most potentially career-threatening thing I have ever done. And yet I do it gladly. I do it because Michael asks it of me, and when he asks, I answer with my obedience. I do it to show my submission to this man I love so very much.

My feet are up on the desk now, the wheels of my chair squeaking rhythmically on the floor as I fuck myself with a piece of fruit. There could be a whole crowd watching me at play, and I wouldn't know. And if I knew, I wouldn't care. As he wanted, as he instructed, I am thinking of him—and only him—as the steady thrusting of the banana and the delicate pressure of my finger on my clit pushes me over the edge.

When my head clears and my knees are steady enough that I can stand up without trembling, I wrap the ruined banana in one of the napkins that came with my sandwich. It will still be there at the end of the day, just as the receipt for Michael's suit will still be in my drawer. I really should remember to collect that dry cleaning, but I'm prepared to suffer the consequences. After all, who knows what I might be having for lunch tomorrow?

WHEN PENNY MET HARRY

Stan Kent

I spotted him the moment he stepped through the doors of the Whip and Rider.

Eye contact! He'd spotted me even though a Friday night deluge crowded the pub with more than its usual quota of office workers and late-night shoppers; standing alone, forlorn, in the corner, I was an easy target for his well-honed female-in-distress radar. Just by the way he sauntered in, I could tell he was a player with a resilient ego. He no doubt believed all gorgeous females were his ordained bedmates who at one time or another he'd had passionate affairs with. They just needed to be reminded of it. He came straight to me and got close. He had no respect for personal space.

"Haven't we fucked before?"

What an opening line. Out of the mouth of a less skilled operator, such a blunt phrase would have been doomed to ridicule, but rolling off his golden tongue the introduction worked like a charm. It didn't hurt that he looked like a young Michael Caine in *Alfie*. He was the whole bad boy, alpha-male package. He was perfect, especially for someone like me with my submissive peccadilloes. I don't think rejection was in his vocabulary; he probably regarded a slap as a come-on. I liked that in a man. So I gave him one.

He didn't flinch; he laughed.

"I'm sorry darlin'. I was only trying to be helpful. You looked like you wanted a good, hard fucking and didn't know how to go about getting it."

He was right, but I decided to be coy. He might have been the one to fulfill my needs, but I wanted more of his cockiness before I got his cock.

"What gives you that idea?"

"You look like you don't hang about in pubs very much. You're standing all uncomfortable-like in a corner, near the toilets, being pushed around by the near-constant stream of drinkers whose bladders need a long-delayed piss. You look posh, dressed smartly in that snappy double-breasted blue trouser suit that suggests you've been on a job interview, or out for some special occasion. The wide-collared white shirt and man's floral tie is a bit too flash to be usual office garb."

He fingered the cloth of my blazer. I imagined his fingers on me.

"These are not mall clothes. You've got lots of cash to flash. At first glance I might have mistaken you for an out-on-the-town dapper young gent, but your feminine attributes stick out through your fancy-boy gloss. Look atchya."

He fingered my hair. I imagined his fingers between my legs.

"Your flouncy golden hair peeks out from underneath that narrow-brimmed floppy hat in a carefully designed attempt to look distressed and vulnerable. Your pink-rouged lips highlight that peaches-and-cream, perfectly innocent complexion. Those dainty high heels jut out from underneath the blue cuffs of your pinstripe trousers, making your arse stick out oh so invitingly. If you were a man, you'd be a bloody attractive one. I'd be tempted to give you one."

He slapped my ass playfully, but with an intent that spoke volumes reminiscent of the Marquis's classics. Oh yes, he was the one.

He put his clenched hand under my chin, lifting my head up to face him.

"Something's upset you. Look at those smudged mascara circles bringing all that attention to the redness of your eyes. That can't be due to the Whip and Rider's smoky atmosphere. You've been crying. No doubt about it."

He ordered a double whiskey, matching the drink I'd been nursing.

"You've probably been stood up for a date or turned down for a job. You don't need cash, or maybe you do; the sharp clothes could be gifts from Mommy and Daddy or better yet, a sugar daddy. You're definitely new to London. You don't have that hardened look that us city dwellers develop after a few months in the smoke and grime of being ready for anything that the Smoke throws atchya. Then there's your drink. You ordered a double whiskey and haven't touched a drop. So here, drink up. Cheers. I do believe this is the start of a beautiful fucking friendship."

"Cheers," I said, not bothering to dispute his conclusion. I took a large gulp of whiskey and winced. He laughed.

"That's better. The name's Harry—Harry Gathers."

"Penelope Crumleigh, and you are very perceptive. I am a little upset."

"This town can do that to you, darlin'. A tip from a London native: roll with the punches, love; don't let the Smoke get the better of you. A little homesick are you?"

"Not really. I lost my job."

"Oh dear, now I see why the double whiskey."

I laughed, a sniffle escaping my nose.

"Yes, it is a little ridiculous isn't it? I thought I owed it to myself to get drunk."

"Happen today did it?"

"No, almost a month ago."

Harry looked incredulous at my extended period of workplace mourning.

"If you don't mind me asking, what kind of biz you in?"

"I'm—I was—a teacher."

"Really? A friend of mine's a teacher. She just got a job."

"Oh, that's good."

I smiled.

"Yeah, took her six months, but—"

My smile slipped into lip quivering as I sniffled back the tears.

"Oh dear, oh dear, I'll never find a—"

Harry put a friendly arm around my quaking shoulders.

"Oh, I'm sorry, Penny. You don't mind me calling you Penny, do you? Can't go on calling you Penelope. It'd be like you calling me Harold. Not even me dear old mum, the devil rest her soul, called me Harold, except when she was angry with me, which happened every now and then on account of me being a likely lad, and nobody's business was that. So you won't mind me calling you Penny because you're a pretty Penny indeed. Penny it is, right you are."

He didn't bother to wait for my response.

"Where were we? Six months—oh yeah, it's just me and my big mouth. Don't you worry. You'll find something soon. There's plenty of temp jobs around that'll keep you going until the right position comes around. I have loads of contacts in all the right places for a pretty young thing like you. Look, why don't we get out of here and talk about it. You look like you need a shoulder to cry on, and mine are guaranteed sympathetic and waterproof. There's a nice bistro around the corner, Le Petite Mort. It's quiet and we can have a good old chin-wag. You'll feel much better after a nice meal and a good cry."

"Okay, thanks. Thanks, Harry. Lead the way. I could use a good talk."

And a good dominating fuck, I said to myself. Finally it looked like I'd found the antidote to the hordes of caring, sensitive males that roamed the dating plains leaving me bored and orgasmless. Harry knocked back his whiskey in one gulp. I did the same, impressing Harry to no end with my wince.

It was two hours and three bottles of generic French Chablis later when the conversation drifted back into job matters. I picked at my crème brûlée. Harry had already devoured his and was lighting up another cigarette. The pre-, during and postprandial conversation had skirted getting-to-know-you pleasantries designed to put me at ease. After all that wine I was feeling no pain.

"Mind if I ask why you lost your job, Penny?"

My words were slurred, but despite Le Petite Mort's ambient din of numerous huddled conversations, I could tell from the smile on Harry's face that he'd deciphered my drunk-speak.

"You might say, sexual harassment."

"You don't say. Were you the harasser or the harassee?"

"Definitely the harassee. And I still have the bruises to prove it. Would you like to see them?"

I stood on shaky feet and fumbled with the snap of my trousers. Despite his alpha-male enthusiasm for an up close and personal view of my pert ass, Harry showed surprising reserve; Le

Petite Mort was just not the place for a Soho striptease, he said. Harry helped me back into my chair and signaled for the bill. I figured it was time to start testing his boundaries with some good old-fashioned cantankerousness.

"What's the matter, Harry, you don't believe me? I thought you were my friend."

"Penny, I am. I am, but we don't want everyone in the restaurant to see, do we?"

I giggled, putting my fingertips to my mouth.

"Oh dear, I forgot—we're in pubic—I mean public. I'm so used to making a spectacle of myself. Do you know twenty businessmen saw my bottom?"

"Really? Why don't we get out of here and make that twenty-one. Where is that waiter? Waiter!"

Harry lay naked on my bed. I was in engaged in the obligatory pre-sex visit to the bathroom, but could eye him through the cracked-open door. Making himself right at home, he sipped a brandy that he'd helped himself to. I flushed the toilet, washed my hands, checked my face and emerged, propping myself up seductively against the wall. Harry looked over the rim of his glass at my shadowy figure. I'd let down my hair. I'd taken off my jacket. The high heels were gone too. I rubbed my stockinged feet nervously together.

"Harry?"

"Yes, Penny."

"What are you going to do to me?"

By the diffuse light of the bedside lamp, I fumbled with my necktie. Harry was pussy-wettingly direct.

"I'm going to tie your hands behind your back and spank you hard before I make you suck my cock. If you're a good little cocksucker then I'll spank you even harder, and then when you're nice and red and tender, I'll fuck you harder, very much harder—in the arse."

A wicked smile spread across Harry's face. I had died and gone to hell, where I belonged, rather than that boring alternative.

"Thank you, Harry. You see, I've been such a naughty girl. I've been very bad and need to be punished. Severely. You must show no mercy."

"I don't know the meaning of the word. Now come over here and take your punishment like a woman."

I slinked to the side of the bed. Harry pulled the tie from my neck, draping the garment over his cock, looping it around and into his hands. He held the tie as if it were the reins of a horse; his cock strained like a stallion ready to burst from the gate. He rubbed himself. I wanted to help him play with his cock, but I was afraid to show any initiative in case he fell into the lazy man's trap of expecting me to do all the work without direction. I *need* firm direction. I was desperate for a man to take charge of my bedroom, and my patience was rewarded by Harry's uncompromising tones.

"Don't just stand there admiring my cock. Take off your trousers, bad Penny. Stand at the foot of the bed and take them off. You've been a naughty girl. I'm going to thrash you. I'm going to spank your pretty little bottom until it is shiny and pink and then watch as it turns black and blue, but first I want to ogle you as you undress. I want you to give me the sluttiest striptease show I've ever seen. Make me want to come just from looking atchya."

"Certainly, Harry. I'll do anything you ask."

I backed away from Harry, my fingers on the zipper and buttons of my pinstriped trousers as I retreated. Harry pulled my tie tighter around his cock, sliding the silk backward and forward to massage his erection. I inched my zipper down and peeled the flaps of the trousers apart. Harry looked closely, but the white shirt covered my flesh. Pushing the waistband down my hips, I wiggled, sticking my bottom backward as the trousers dropped down my thighs to pool around my ankles in a crinkled heap. I stepped out of the trousers, kicking them aside with my stocking-covered toe. The white shirt draped low to my thighs, almost reaching the tops of the stay-up black stockings that came above my knee. Harry whistled.

"You are a naughty girl, Penny, dressing like a whore for a job interview. Take off your shirt, naughty Miss Penny whore."

"Yes, Harry, but I have a confession to make. I wasn't on a job interview. I was on the job. You're right to call me a whore because I've become one since losing my teaching position."

A smile crept across Harry's face. He looked truly pleased to know that I was a professional woman.

"That's lovely. That's the best news I've heard all day. You're going to save me lots of trouble. I have just the job for you, and to get you ready for it I'm going to teach you a few new positions tonight, Miss Penny whore. I knew it when I saw you. I said, 'Harry, there's a girl who wouldn't mind being paid to fuck and beat old geezers.' We're a marriage made in heaven and hell, Miss Penny whore, because I'm a gentleman pimp looking for a high-class lady like you, but before I accept you into my exclusive stable you've got to prove yourself. Now what are you stalling for? Strip for me. Make my cock harder than it's ever been, all the harder to fuck you with."

How wonderful. I did not have to be ashamed of what I'd become. I undid the buttons of my shirt one by excruciating one, beginning with the cuffs, then moving to the neck, and descending down to the very last one that hovered in the vicinity of my cunt. Arching my arms backward, I let the garment fall from my body. Harry gasped his approval. My skin was as white as the shirt, contrasting sharply with the jet black of the bra, my camisole panties and opaque stockings.

Harry was breathing harder.

"Show me your tits, whore."

"Yes, Harry, I'll show you my whore's breasts."

"Tits."

"Yes, I'll show you my whore's tits."

"That's better, now you're learning."

I reached behind and unsnapped the push-up bra. Shrugging my shoulders, I let the lacy object fall forward and join the shirt and trousers.

"Pinch your tits, whore. Make your whore's nipples hard for me so that when I spank you, you'll be able to feel them rub against my cock—that you've made so hard, you little slut."

Harry's brusque manner and crude language reminded me of my younger days at the country estate where Cousin Geoffrey had been forced to discipline me for leading the gardener astray. I spoke in a little girl voice.

"Yes, Harry. I'll make them very hard for your cock."

I gripped my nipples between my thumb and forefingers and pulled my small, firm breasts forward into fleshy cones. I twisted my nipples in circular motions, my golden areolae and pale breast flesh following in enticing spirals behind the dark brown nubs. I could tell my slutty display pleased and amazed Harry. We were meant for each other.

"Come over here, you bad girl, Penny. You're a natural tease. You belong in a dive bar stripping for rowdy men. You must be punished for being a whore who plays with her tits to get men so excited. Get yourself over here and fast."

"Yes, Harry. Punish me. Teach me to be a good girl who comes when bad men fuck her."

Harry looked puzzled over my last comment, not knowing that I can't come unless I'm dominated, and most men are too afraid to take control, especially on the first date and/or the first fuck. I need a bad man, and Harry was a skilled, smooth operator who righteously fell into that category. He would soon enough figure out my peccadilloes. As I hoped, realization dawned on his face as I bounded over to him, pulling at my breasts as I ran. I dived across his lap as he propped himself up in the bed with a few pillows, and my breasts collided with his erection. My nipples were rock hard as they glided across his cock.

"Put your hands behind your back. I'm going to tie your hands so tight that you can't struggle, and no matter how much you beg me, I won't go easy on you."

Harry took the silk tie and knotted it around my wrists, securing the bond tight. He hooked his fingers into the waistband of my black camisole panties, but before he slid them down my slender hips, he paused.

"Before you can be punished, you must confess."

My little girl voice returned with just a hint of Victorian melodrama thrown in for good measure.

"Oh shame, shame. Must I tell you all?"

"Yes, you must tell me everything."

Harry's cock pulsed against my breasts; I rubbed them across his glans, making my nipples harder with every brush of his cockhead.

"Oh Harry, men pay me to spank them. I am horrible. I enjoy it tremendously. I love watching their come shoot across the room as I spank their bottoms. I'm such a filthy whore, aren't I?"

"Yes, yes, Penny whore, you are, and I shall punish you for taking advantage of these poor helpless men, and after that you will agree to do anything I ask."

"Oh yes, but punish me hard. Don't go easy. Do your best of your worst. I'll do whatever you ask, Harry. Just spank me very hard. I must pay for all the men I've punished. That's why I was crying in the pub. I'd just finished beating a man and had been paid very well for it too. I left his flat feeling so aroused and filthy. They never make me come. I beat them, but I want to be beaten. They come and then it's over. I leave and have to play with myself to get rid of the nasty feelings in my pussy. I sometimes can't wait until I get home. I go to the nearest filthy bathroom and masturbate myself to orgasm. I need punishing too. I need punishing until I come. Oh punish me hard, Harry, spank me into submission."

Harry's fingers peeled down my knickers. The luxurious material stuck between my damp thighs. I was wetter than the London weather. Showing the ideal temperament that I crave, he tired of my panties sticking between my thighs. With a sudden strength that took my breath away, he tore the sodden silky garment from its sticky trap. He stroked the pert globes of my bottom. He traced the faint bruises on my otherwise perfect skin, whistling his appreciation for the last punishment I received. The bruises had faded and needed to be refreshed, and Harry was just the man to bring back the black, blue and purple badge of honor I wear with pride.

"Punish you hard, Miss Penny whore? Hard? Is that what you want? Like this?"

Harry gave me no chance to answer. His hand came down on my arse more dramatically than forcefully. I felt my bottom ripple, sending a slight shock wave through my body and onto Harry's cock. It felt glorious to me, and by the way his cock twitched its appreciation, Harry too must have enjoyed the thrill.

"I am going to spank you harder, Miss Penny whore, because

you spank those poor pathetic men who pay you large amounts of cash to spank them harder than they deserve. I shall hit you harder because you are such a naughty girl. You're a spanking whore, and I shall reward you for it in the manner to which you shall become accustomed."

Harry's palm came down with a reverberating crack on my punishable posterior. My head shot back. My bottom tensed in resistance. The pain was immediate and exquisite. Harry's cock throbbed.

"Yes, yes, like that. More, Harry, spank me more. Punish wicked Penelope."

"How did you become such a spanking whore, naughty Penny?"

Harry punctuated his question with a loud slap. During my answer, he smoothed the rapidly reddening flush of my ass-cheeks, his wandering fingers brushing the pout of my inflamed mons, dipping deeply to coat his fingers with the wetness of my pussy. I was dripping for him.

"After losing my teaching job I came to London. I stopped in a telephone box outside of the train station to call for a place to stay. Inside the box were all these small cards from women—whores—advertising their services."

For the next spank, Harry smeared my cunt juice over my rosy arsecheeks, making them tingle even more.

"Hooker cards."

"Yes, yes, that's what they are called. Many advertise spanking and similar perversions. I'd lost my job because I'd acted like a slutty whore, so I felt as if I was fated to become one. I rented this flat and advertised—a plain card, no picture, offering *Naughty Schoolteacher Gives Punishment to Rude Schoolboys.* My phone hasn't stopped ringing. There are so many men who want to be spanked."

"And not enough naughty whores who do their job well."

"Then I have found my true calling and as a reward you must spank me harder."

"I shall spank you harder, and your reward will be to know that it is allowable to spank these useless men for buckets of cash as long as you then submit to me. The scales will be balanced. For you to be a happy Penny you need to give and receive a spanking; your ass tells me so."

He had read me so well, and he was completely right. I could continue my spanking career as long as I too was punished. I suddenly felt so liberated. With each blow, I squirmed across his lap, pressing his throbbing erection tight against my stomach, inciting him to do more nasty things to me. Instead of pulling his fingers out of my pussy, Harry lingered inside of me, so that when he smacked my arse he no doubt felt the blow travel through my cheeks, to my pussy and onto his fingers. I had never felt anything like this; the added vibrations inside me made me shake and writhe, my bottom and thighs tensing on his fingers. I howled.

"Harry, spank me harder, I'm coming. Make me come. Make your Penny whore come. Call me a whore, please, please."

"Whore, whore, whore, whore—"

"Yes, yes, yes I am. I am a naughty little whore. Oh, yes, yes, yes I am. I am coming. You're making your Penny whore come on you fingers."

Harry's hand rained down on my bottom as his clenched fingers slid in and out of my cunt. I arched my back with each blow to heighten the stinging impact, flopping wildly as I orgasmed over his coaxing digits. Harry continued to spank me as pounding climaxes consumed my being. Weeks of frustrated sexual tension were released from me in a single moment.

After several minutes' respite, Harry stroked my head,

knotting his fingers in my hair. He pulled my head backward and kissed it.

"Your punishment isn't complete, Miss Penny whore. You must drink my come. I enjoy a good cocksucking, and something tells me you are primed to satisfy."

"Nothing will give me a greater pleasure. I am an excellent cocksucker."

"I'll be the judge of your oral abilities, wench."

I slid off of Harry's lap and onto my knees. Hands tied behind my back, I stumbled to stand on wobbly legs, eventually diving headlong onto the bed between Harry's feet.

He watched my progress with a detached air, to my relief never once offering any gentlemanly assistance. I was overcome with extreme pleasure to be left to my own silly devices, to not hear a pathetic, "Oh, let me help you." Without the aid of my hands, I used my chin and breasts as props, crawling between his legs, pausing at his crotch, licking the sagging flesh of his balls.

"May I suck you, Harry?"

"Only if you suck well."

"I shall try, but if I do not meet your standards, please correct me. Punish me into becoming a better cocksucker."

Harry grabbed my golden locks and tipped my head back. My mouth bobbed open. A stream of spittle hung down from my lower lip to his balls.

"Have no doubt that I'll improve your sucking, woman. Now stop filling your mouth with useless words and eat my cock. Eat my cock, and afterward you must tell me all. Your punishment is not complete until you confess every one of your sins. I want to hear all the dirty things you've done. If you're to work for me and be rewarded with regular punishments, there can be no secrets."

Using a handful of my golden hair, Harry pushed my head
into his lap and guided his cock into my mouth. Knotting my
hair around his fist, Harry manipulated my head up and down
his shaft, my lips working magic along his trembling length. I
could tell it would not be long until he erupted.

"Suck, whore, suck, whore, suck, whore...."

Harry's chanting matched every cycle of my pumping mouth.
With my hands bound behind me, I couldn't support myself. My
mouth gravitated to the base of Harry's cock, my face buried
in his musky pubic nest. As I writhed and arched to perform a
most excellent sucking, I thought not only of his erection and
its impending release, but also of being fucked in the arse as I
sucked him off. Just like I had in my last job. Perhaps Harry had
a client who would oblige me the favor? Thinking of such divine
degradation, I climaxed. I ground my pussy into the bedcovers.
As Harry came, he reached for my head and pulled me from his
orgasming cock by my hair, his stream of milky jism splattering
in my face. I lapped at the liquid as if his coming on my pretty
facial features was a special honor.

It was.

Harry had no idea that in coming on my face he'd fulfilled
my special fantasy of being degraded. At that moment I realized
my true sluttish nature. Harry had vindicated my decision to
follow my slutty self. My life in London was just a reflection of
my whorish past, like that first glimpse I'd received at Cousin
Geoffrey's estate all those years ago in my childhood. Just as he
had punished me for being such a wanton slut; so had Harry.
My life had gone full circle; I was home, where I belonged.

With his come dripping from my mouth and nose, I looked
straight at Harry as he held my head aloft by my luxurious
golden mop. I spoke softly.

"Spank me again, Harry. Fuck me in the arse and spank my

bottom, and I'll tell you my sordid tale."

"My pleasure."

I didn't bother to correct Harry that the pleasure was mine too. I was too happy. Stretching into the pale, gray dawn of another London morning, and beyond, he filled the missing parts of my libido. We were Yin and Yang, Spanker and Spankee, Fucker and Fuckee; Harry possessed me like no man ever had the power to do. In return I was glad to give him the perfect woman to use in his high-class escort service for upper-class gentlemen and ladies, because finally I had a gentleman who knew how to treat me wrong.

THE POWER OF NO

Teresa Noelle Roberts

D on't come," Enrique ordered. "Whatever I do to you tonight, you are not to come without permission."

And then he showed me the rawhide flogger.

I laughed and said, "As if!"

I'd come lying across his lap as he spanked me, my bare mound grinding against his muscled thigh, my ass rising to meet his hand, then falling back so I could press against him. That was glorious pain, warm and rose-pink and not much like pain in the usual sense at all. More like the familiar rough edges of a vigorous fuck, of having my nipples twisted to a delicious ache, of being bent into odd positions until my muscles screamed for mercy and I ignored them because the cock pounding hard and fierce into me was just too intoxicating.

That kind of pain.

Flogging, though, stung, like paper cuts and lemon juice on a much larger scale. Depending on how hard he was in-spired to strike, it stung a lot. At least it did with that rawhide flogger. And since I was a new bottom—brash and impatient and inclined to push myself and find out how much I could really take—I'd ended up, on my first encounter with it, with an ass that felt like I'd sat on a red ants' nest.

It had been fun in a weird way. I'd struggled and shrieked and yelped and begged for mercy that I didn't really want, at least not enough to use my safeword. When he'd stopped, though, I realized I was dripping wet and as soon as he thrust into me, I'd come, screaming and sobbing and more than a little confused.

But while the flogging was going on, I was in no danger of coming.

Which is why I responded as sarcastically as I did.

I realized almost immediately I'd made a mistake.

Enrique has a great sense of humor. But it's one thing to laugh with one's dom and another to laugh at him—and inexperienced though I was, I knew I'd crossed a line, a knowledge confirmed when he chuckled in a melodrama-villain way and said, "Oh, you're in trouble now!" He pretended to twirl his black moustache, which fortunately wasn't long enough to twirl. His dark eyes looked amused rather than annoyed—thank goodness for that—but there was something distinctly sadistic in the amusement, like he loved his work with the Spanish Inquisition and was relishing this new, mouthy heretic.

I leaned against the bed and braced myself for pain, rolling my safeword silently on my tongue so it would be ready when I needed it. I hadn't yet, in our first month of playing, but there was a first time for everything and this seemed likely to be it. I'd goaded him, after all.

"When you're about to come, say 'edge,'" he commanded. "I'll let you know if you may. Now don't move. I want to see how well you hold position. And don't come without permission."

Too nervous to laugh this time—and, I was convinced, too

anxious to need to worry about coming—I took a deep breath
and waited for my ass to catch fire.

Instead, I felt the flogger glide across the skin of my back, a
sensual caress. It didn't feel like the stiff strands I'd been antici-
pating, either, but something softer, suede perhaps.

That bastard had switched floggers on me! I itched to turn
around and see which he'd chosen. I hadn't seen even a fraction
of Enrique's toy collection, and curiosity was trying to get the
better of me. Those falls felt so velvety as they brushed across
my back, making my skin twitch like a cat's in their wake, sending shivers deep into my core. Maybe they *were* velvet, or perhaps fur? I wanted to know....

But I couldn't make myself turn around.

I told myself it was because I didn't want to spoil whatever
game he was playing. I wanted to know, but I certainly didn't
want him to stop, and I risked that if I turned around, since he'd
told me to hold still.

That was what I told myself, anyway.

The flogger trailed lower, teasing my ass briefly, then moving
to my thighs. It almost tickled, and I fought the urge to squirm
and shiver.

But I had to do or say something. Erotic tension was pooling
between my legs, swelling my nipples, and I wouldn't be able
to hold still much longer under the gentle tickling. "Please," I
begged. "Please flog me."

"You want me to flog you? I thought you didn't like it. You
laughed when I suggested you might come from it."

"Please..." I took a deep breath and in that second managed to organize my thoughts a bit. "I'm not sure I could
come from it, but I do like it. And what you're doing...tick-
les." The last word came out on a shriek, because, as if he read
my mind, Enrique quivered the flogger on the sensitive skin of

my side, making me want to flinch and jump and dance.

But I didn't.

Enrique noticed. "Good girl," he said quietly.

I flushed with pride, and then flushed even deeper when I realized I was doing it. "Good girl"—like I was a kid, or a dog, and still it went to my head.

And my pussy. I was wet, I realized, far more wet than I could explain from the bit of playing we'd done so far, and the quiet "Good girl" had a lot more to do with that than I was sure I liked.

And as I was contemplating that, the flogger danced across my ass.

A far softer sensation than the rawhide thongs, it stung and thumped, but almost simultaneously soothed its own sting with a whispering caress.

Oh God, I could get used to this!

I thrust my ass back in invitation.

Then said, "Oh, shit! I'm sorry."

Enrique ran his hand down the curve of my hip, the line of my flank. "You caught yourself, though. And if you must move, I'd rather see you wriggling in pleasure than trying to squirm away." Unexpectedly, he smacked my ass with his hand, hard, making me yelp in surprise, but at the same time sending a bolt of fire directly to my clit. "But from now on, hold still."

Somehow, I managed not to jump.

I was rewarded with another pussy-clenching, "Good girl."

And then he turned again to the flogger.

Stinging and thuddy and silken, it teased sensation out of me, making my ass throb deliciously and my pussy throb to its rhythm.

After only a few minutes, I felt swollen, larger than life, and the longer he went on, the more I ached with lust. "Edge," I

hissed through my teeth, knowing all I'd have to do was contract my cunt muscles once, or shift so my slick lips slid over my
clit, and I'd be off like a rocket.

"No," Enrique said, and changed the soft flogger for the
more stinging one I'd experienced before. I hadn't cared for the
sensation that first time, but now, aroused almost beyond sanity
by the long dance with soft suede, it felt like the erotic equivalent of a hot Thai curry, fierce but delicious.

For the first few strokes, the sharp bites were a welcome respite, arousing, but different enough from the earlier sensation
that it was almost as if Enrique had hit an arousal-reset button.

That didn't last long, though. Soon, I was soaring again,
feeling as if my brain and my self-respect had fallen into my
wet, greedy pussy and were lost forever.

I needed. Needed Enrique's cock in me. Needed a sharper
jolt of pain. Needed, more than ever, to come. I bit the inside
of my cheek, hoping to distract myself, but that bit of pain just
fueled the fire.

"Edge. Please."

"Not yet," Enrique said, and stepped up the pace of the flogging, striking a bit harder, a bit faster, catching the sensitive
flesh of my thighs, the area Enrique called "the sweet spot,"
instead of my ass.

"Edge. Please. Edge. Please, please let me come…" From a
plea, I made it into a prayer—but once again, I was denied.

And perversely, the denial went straight to my clit, putting
me in even worse straits.

My body throbbed, aching to come, or failing that, to dance
and squirm under the blows and release a little of the tension
coiling inside me. Instead, I counted to twenty in French, and
then in Spanish. Then to ten in German, which was all I could
remember.

The effort distracted me just enough. I still felt like I might become a victim of spontaneous human combustion if I didn't get off soon, but I'd gotten past the critical seconds where I thought I might lose control.

Using the handle of the flogger, Enrique nudged my legs farther apart.

I held my breath in anticipation. Maybe now, at last, he'd fuck me, and I'd be allowed to come on his cock.

"Edge," I begged on a sighing breath.

"No." Enrique's voice was so stern that I flinched. I didn't shift my position, but I could feel my muscles twitch and shift under my skin.

More gently, he added, "You're doing really well. Such a good, obedient girl."

I thought I'd been hot already, but those words made me molten. My few remaining brain cells made a note to try to work through why, because while it's always nice to be praised, I was astonished by my intense, intensely sexual reaction. Oh, I knew in theory that some people took joy in obedience, becoming putty in someone's hands...but I'd never pegged myself for one of them, just a straightforward sensation slut.

I'd figure that out later. Much, much later. Right now, I just wanted to bask in the feeling.

"Don't move and ruin it," he said, putting one big hand on the back of my head, emphasizing I was to stay put, stay leaning against the bed with my head bowed. The feel of that hand, that weight, that authority keeping me in place, was almost too much, almost pushed me over the edge. It didn't make a whole lot of sense at the time, but neither could I deny the sudden contraction of my pussy, or the lava flow between my legs, or the strange tug on my heart that just added to the sensations.

But I fought back against it. He'd praised me for being good and obedient, and good and obedient I would stay if it killed me.

Then he struck at the sensitive inside of my thigh, clasping the back of my neck harder as he did as if reminding me to obey. It hurt, but in my current state it was a glorious pain.

Once, twice, three times, and with each, I shrieked, with increasing desperation, "Edge!" By the third, there were tears of pure frustration running down my face, but I couldn't— wouldn't—let go without permission. Couldn't disappoint him.

Couldn't disappoint myself.

On the fourth strike, I just broke down and blubbered, "Pleasepleaseplease."

"Do you want to come?" Enrique asked calmly, as if I hadn't been begging for it for what seemed like hours.

I nodded, whimpered a few more pleases and thank yous.

He set the whip down on the bed, put both his hands on my shoulders. "Then come for me," he demanded. "Now."

And without any direct touch, with nothing but his word, I came so hard my knees buckled, came so hard I sobbed, came so hard that for a few seconds I couldn't see or breathe and the pleasure was almost painful in its intensity.

"I've got you," Enrique said, easing me down onto the bed. He curled up around me and cuddled me close as I came down.

And just when I was finally sure I wasn't going to become the first documented case of death by orgasm, his hard cock slipped between my legs, teasing and nudging at my engorged, sensitive pussy lips. Instantly I was aroused again, wanting him in me, wanting to come again. I pushed back against him, begging for more. Begging to be fucked.

"Not yet," he said. "Not yet."

He had me whimpering "Edge" again as his cock teased at me without entering. This time, though, I knew I could take it, knew I could hold out.

Until he rolled me over onto hands and knees, entered me fast and hard.

I screamed "Edge," felt the first shimmers of orgasm wash over me, tried to hold it back.

"Now!" Enrique ordered, pounding into me.

I howled and obeyed.

Later—much later, when we'd showered and were curled up together on Enrique's couch, half-eaten containers of pad thai and massaman curry in front of us—Enrique kissed the top of my head and said, a little awe in his voice, "I didn't expect you to hold out so long."

"I'm stubborn," I said, "and I hate to lose." But I knew that wasn't the whole story, and so did Enrique.

"That'll do a lot," he said. "But I saw your face when I said how good and obedient you were. That got under your skin, didn't it?"

As I nodded, I could feel myself blushing. "I liked...the sense of being controlled, and I liked knowing you were pleased with me. I wanted to come so badly, but I didn't want to let you down. That seemed more important than what I wanted."

Enrique smiled a smile that fluttered straight to my groin. "I thought you had it in you, for all you thought you were only interested in a little sensation play."

"Have what in me?" I asked, although I had some inkling. My heart and body seemed to know already; it was just my brain that was having a little trouble with the concept.

"Submission. Wanting to give your will up to me, at least some of the time. Needing to be controlled. To obey. To be told no sometimes..."

"Because it makes you happy—and because it makes the yes that much better when you give it," I said. "That much I get from tonight. The rest...it's a little scary, but intriguing."

"Intriguing enough to explore further?"

"Hell yes!" I thought about it for about ten seconds more. "As long as I'm not going to always be denied orgasms, because I think that could get really old."

"Only when I feel like it," Enrique chuckled. "Only when I feel like it."

And that answer, ominous as it was—or maybe for that very reason—was good enough for me.

IN THE CORNER

Sommer Marsden

Frankie is a nice guy. He holds the door for me. He orders wine with dinner. He always notices my outfit and my hair, even jewelry. Frankie bores the fuck out of me.

We'd just come from dinner. He suggested Dorian's for a drink. I agreed. Maybe the crowded, smoky ambience would be enough to give the evening a little electroshock therapy. Wake things up a bit. Maybe the noise and the booze would suppress my urge to chew my own wrists open. Frankie is a nice, boring guy.

Dorian's was incredibly crowded. As usual, the Friday night crowd had worked itself into a frenzy. Loud music, loud men, drunken women. Good stuff. I found two stools in the corner and perched there in my short, black baby-doll dress and black hose. I hooked my heels on the stool's bottom bar and waited. I needed a drink. Badly.

I spotted Frankie moving through the crowd, two beers high above his head, a determined look on his face. Good, my drink was on its way.

"Amelia the Great." The voice snaked into my ear and the hair on my nape rose with excitement. I knew that voice. I knew that voice very well. It had called me many names and given many directions. It had instructed me to do filthy, nasty things. I loved that voice.

"Richard," I said before I even turned fully on the stool. "How are you?"

It was hard to keep my voice all cool and aloof. Harder still to fight the rise of color in my cheeks. Impossible to control the automatic seize of my nipples as they stood at attention just at the sound of that dark, gruff voice.

"Nice dress." His deep blue eyes scanned me like he owned me. Once upon a time, he had. The urge to obey welled up in me fast and full.

"Thank you." I waved a hand to Frankie, who was still fighting the crowd.

"Have anything on under there?" he whispered directly in my ear and hooked a finger under the hem.

I pushed my hand against his to stop him, though the action fought my very nature. When my hand touched his, I felt my body let loose a slow trickle of moist heat between my legs.

"Yes. I do." My voice was doing that shaking thing. I sounded like I was about to cry. I wasn't. I was just incredibly turned on and fighting it with everything I had.

"Well, people do change," he laughed. When he laughed, his face changed. He still looked threatening, but in a good way. A bad boy who would make you do bad things and make you love every last minute of it. My heart slammed in my chest and I took a deep breath.

"The dress is short," I explained, still clutching the hem, though he had removed his finger.

"Damn straight it is. I saw you come in. Don't drop anything on the floor or we'll all get a show. Me personally, I'm praying you spill the contents of your purse everywhere." When he said it, he slid the tip of his finger along my spine. I shivered.

"I'm here with someone." I wanted to sound cool and confident. I failed. It came out like a guilty confession. Fast and awkward.

"So I see. Not really your type, is he?" he said, keeping his eyes on Frankie, who had been stopped by a man I recognized as one of his friends from work.

"He's..." I watched Frankie, too, and I suddenly hated him. Hated his quiet, polite ways. His manners. How gentle he was with me in bed. As if I would break. He had never put tiny jeweled clamps on my nipples until I wanted to beg for removal. He had never given me twenty lashings with a whip until my body contorted with pleasure and pain. He had never punished me or spanked me or made me crawl around the house five paces behind him.

But to be fair, Frankie didn't know my kinks. I hadn't told him. I didn't want to. Because Frankie was boring and I was trying to be "normal."

"An amusement," Richard finished for me. "He wouldn't know what to do with you even if you were honest with him."

"Not everyone is like you," I said softly. A little fear shot through me at my bold tone. That didn't stop my body from responding to the malicious smile on his full lips. My body had been well conditioned to respond to Richard at his cruelest. This was nothing. I shifted on the stool, praying it looked as if I were simply uncomfortable.

"True. Very few are like me." He openly watched me shifting. Grinning even wider, he slid his hand up my thigh. "What's wrong, Amelia? Are you wet in those proper panties? I bet you are. How wet are you?"

I couldn't stop him. I don't think I would have if I could. He slid his hand under the short hem and past my thigh-high hose. He slid a finger under my thong and pushed his big finger into the wetness that pooled there. It happened so fast. And no one saw. No one but me.

My breath solidified in my lungs and I squirmed on the end of his finger. A worm on a hook. A puppet on a string.

"I see. You still soak yourself when you want something." His mouth was right next to my ear and it sent sparkles of alternating cold and hot along my skin. He bit the top of my ear hard and I felt my cunt constrict around his finger. "And you're still into the pain," he laughed. "That hasn't changed."

Frankie finally arrived, clutching the beers with a victorious grin. Until he saw where Richard's hand was. Until he took in my heaving chest and my face, which I could feel was flushed and hot. Still, Frankie was too nice to say anything. Nothing. He looked away, as if to give us time to collect ourselves.

I pitied him and hated him. And I hated myself because the moment I had seen it register in his eyes, the knowledge of what we were doing, a tiny flicker had worked through my pussy. A lovely precursor to the orgasm I already knew I would have.

Richard played along. With a soft snicker, he removed his hand from my body and my dress. Then he introduced himself to Frankie, who had the good manners to respond when Richard offered his hand. The hand that had just been under my dress.

"Richard. Nice to meet you, Frankie. Amelia and I are old friends."

"I see," Frankie said softly and handed me my beer.

That was it. That was all he said. I took a sip of beer and waited. How would this go?

"That was Chuck from the office," Frankie said to me. He looked uncomfortable but determined.

I nodded. "I saw."

Richard finished off the beer he had been holding and bent as if to kiss me. Instead, he said, "In the corner."

My spine straightened and my nipples grew harder still. They ached for the pain I knew he was capable of. The soothing afterward. My skin seemed to pulse and I felt another rush of my own heat between my legs. I scanned the bar and stood without a word. So well conditioned was I. I didn't think but obeyed. I started toward the far left corner of the room.

As if from far away, I heard Richard say, "You don't mind if I borrow her for a few minutes, do you, Frankie? Of course you don't. You're such a nice guy."

I didn't want to give myself away. I didn't want Richard to be able to see the increasing need and want for him in my gait. I failed. I could feel the way I was walking. A sultry, rolling swagger that I'm sure screamed *Fuck me!* to anyone paying attention. And Richard was paying attention. I could feel his eyes singeing the bare skin above the zipper of my dress. I could feel his presence as surely as I could feel the nervous, anxious flutter in my belly. That odd feeling that is somewhere between excitement and sickness.

I went to the back left corner of Dorian's. A little nook right beyond the jukebox. There had once been a pay phone tucked in the corner, but after the fifth time someone had used the receiver during a bar fight, management had removed it. Now, what was there was a useless little dent in the wall. Just big enough for a person.

Without a word, I walked right into it and faced the wall. I was a good girl. I remembered the rules and I followed them. It didn't matter, nor would I mention that I felt like I was being electrocuted. That my skin and my hair and my insides felt charged and sizzling.

He pushed right up against me. No preamble at all. But that's
Richard. Big. He is big all over. Strong and greedy and cruel and
beautiful. My breath rushed out of me as he pushed all of himself against me. His cock was already hard. I felt it ride the seam
of my ass, the pressure of hard flesh against me both threatening
and gorgeous. I shivered but I wasn't cold.

"He is as weak as watered-down scotch," he growled in
my ear and laughed. "Pussy. What are you doing with a pussy,
Amelia the Great?" He shoved his hands under my dress and
pinched the naked skin of my ass. The back string of my thong
left my asscheeks completely exposed above my stockings.

I felt tears sting my eyes even as the first stab of pain coursed
through me and my cunt began to pulse. "I..." He pinched me
again and I lost my words.

"Amelia the Great with a milquetoast man. Who would have
thought it? Certainly not me. I know you like your men brutal."

"Amelia the Great" was Richard's little joke. He would call
me that as he fucked my mouth. He would call me that before
each stroke with the belt. He'd shout it in my face as I crawled
behind him on the floor. Every once in a while, he would sigh
it in my ear as I came. I just never knew when. And I liked it
that way.

Richard yanked the back of my thong, hitching it high between my thighs and against my sex. It felt like I would split in
half but the sopping wet fabric tickled my painfully swollen clit
and I bucked against the dirty green wall.

"See, if I could get you in a corner somewhere more private, I'd be spanking the merry hell out of you right now," he
growled. "Turning that perfect pale ass seven shades of red with
a little purple just for fun."

Another pinch and I sobbed against the wall, my own noise
flung back at me by layers and layers of old paint.

"I could take off my belt and stripe you like a zebra. Throw some painful little jeweled clamps on your rosy red nipples. Make you suck my cock while I pulled your hair. Sadly," he sighed, biting my ear again and pinching my ass, "that would get me arrested in mixed company."

I pushed myself against the wall. Too many things at once. My body couldn't keep up—the pain, the pleasure. I felt dizzy and I wanted him to fuck me. I didn't care that we shared the bar with two hundred others. I wanted him to fuck me in the corner. And he knew it.

Richard switched tactics. His fingertips found my nipples through my dress and he used them instead of clamps. Sandwiching the peaks between his thumbs and forefingers, he bore down hard until spots appeared in my vision. He bit the back of my neck hard enough for me to jump under him even as he pushed his erection against my ass. I pushed back. Bold and whorish and beyond caring.

More pressure; harder and harder he pinched my nipples until I thought I might scream. Then he released me and I sobbed at the thumping pleasure of release as the blood rushed back into my flesh. His hands dove back under my dress and he yanked the back strap of my thong until I heard it tear. Even over the loud music, I heard it give way.

He pushed against the middle of my back and levered me forward. Another searing pinch was administered to my bottom and I felt my pussy go liquid for him. His zipper sounded in my ear and the fact that he was going to fuck me in the corner sunk in. A blip of fear shot up my torso but it was quickly followed by a flood of excitement.

He would fuck me the way he always had, only right here in the middle of the mayhem.

"What about your date?" he chuckled, pushing the head of

his cock just far enough into me to tease. "Are we leaving him out? Should I invite him to watch?"

My skin tingled and the room seemed to be moving. I nodded because as bad as it sounds, I liked the idea. I pushed back against him and he gave me another brutal pinch that had my cunt clenching even as he thrust into me.

"I should, shouldn't I?" he grunted, pounding me so hard I hit my forehead on the wall.

I didn't care. I could deal with that later. His cock skewered me. In, up, high and deep. I felt like I would split in two but each time the pleasure started to crest, he'd slow and pluck at my flesh until I squirmed.

"Should I call him over, so I can teach him what you like? How you are? What you want?"

I nodded, nodded, nodded dumbly to every word. Yes, we could do that. Whatever he wanted. Call him over, let him watch, teach him a thing or two. Every single one of those flitted through my mind as he fucked me.

Richard yanked against my hips, pulling me back onto him even as he rammed into me. His fingers bit deep into my flesh and I knew I would carry the bruises of his long fingers for days. I also knew that I would look at them and touch them often.

His hips pistoned and I felt like I would fall, but he wrapped his arm around me and he held me firm. His other hand snaking back under my dress, he gave a final brutal thrust and pinched my clit so hard it felt like I was being bitten.

I came out loud. I cried and screamed against the green wall with all of Dorian's behind me. I went from rigid in my orgasm to limp in his arms, like a marionette whose strings had been snipped.

He gave me a moment. He wasn't that cruel. I hung there, panting, draped over his arm like a toy he had been too rough with.

"Ready?" he said in my ear. His voice was not only harsh but pleased. I had done well. Or so it seemed.

I stood and let him smooth my dress back over my ass. Richard grabbed the front of my dress like a yoke and pulled me back to my date, his control over me obvious to anyone paying attention.

"Here you go, Frank, my man. Thanks for the loan." He winked and started to turn away.

Frankie was a blazing shade of plum. His hands shook, his mouth a tight seam. God help me, I smiled at him. Even as he stewed in anger and embarrassment, my body hummed with pleasure and satisfaction as I reclaimed the bar stool. The echoes of pain and orgasm in my nipples, my ass, my cunt.

With a final glance over his shoulder, Richard said, "I'll be calling you, Amelia. I didn't realize how much I missed having you around. How much I missed sending you to the corner."

Then he laughed again because he had been the one to cut me loose. The sound skittered under my skin. I nodded my shameless agreement and shifted on my stool some more. He would call. I would answer. There was no doubt.

"I guess I should take you home," Frankie said. "It doesn't seem as if I'm your kind of guy, after all." He looked angry and sad. There was shame in there, too. For me or for him? I wasn't sure.

"No. You're not. Sometimes I wish you were," I said, watching Richard fade back into the crowd, the mixture of excitement and sickness as strong as ever. "But most times, I don't. I like guys who put me in the corner."

STUCK AT WORK AND LATE FOR A DATE

Chelsea Summers

The secretary was bent over the desk with her skirt bunched up over her back and her panties pooled by her feet. Her breathing was strained and she tried to look at the wall clock by her left side, praying that her lateness wouldn't be noticed. Her cheap rayon H&M blouse was pushed carelessly up her chest, exposing her breasts, which had been pulled out and over the top of her beige bra.

Binder clips were cruelly pinching her nipples.

"Keep facing forward," she heard from behind her, and then the soft whoosh of the rolling chair's wheels on the industrial carpet. She flinched in blind preparation; she knew something painful was going to happen, but she wasn't sure what.

There was the clank and rustle of something to the right and behind her. The metal cup and rack that held her office tools. She knew the sound well.

The scratch of the open stapler. The bite of the staple remover. The relentless nip of the binder clips. The smack of the ruler. The poke and scrape of the letter opener. The smooth hardness of the RECEIVED stamp in her asshole. She knew them all, knew them well, wore the memory of the perverted use of these quotidian implements on her flesh like shameful, naughty undergarments.

"Lift your ass toward me," said the voice behind her. Not angry, not passionate. Not anything. Its tone could be requesting her to pass the salt.

Swack! She jumped involuntarily when the ruler hit the back of her thigh. A purple stripe of pain illuminated her head for a moment and faded, though her right thigh still rang with the hurt.

"What do you say?" the voice intoned.

"Yes, Sir," she intoned, and felt her face flush a bit pink. She had forgotten the complex linguistic rules. When she heard "ass," she had to respond "Sir." When she heard "pussy," she had to respond "Master." When she heard "you," she had to respond "Boss." When she heard "whore" or "slut," she had to respond "Daddy." And when she heard none of these words, she had to keep quiet.

It was hard to remember sometimes. It was meant to be hard. It was made to trick her, and trick her it did. It had been created to make her err, and err she did. She often needed correction.

The secretary lifted her ass, tilted it up and back just a little bit, for that was all she could move. Her panty hose had been cut from stem to stern; they now hung in tatters around her thighs. Her ankles had been bound to the legs of the desk with packing tape and her long legs spread in a wide *V* on the acrylic desk mat; her hands leaned far forward on the desk's laminate surface.

She felt the desk's center drawer open against her thighs, a cool sliver of metal. She wished she could turn and press her burning thigh against its smooth, chilly surface. She knew she couldn't, and froze her body, uncomfortably spread and tilted, and felt warm breath on her thigh and heard the metallic rustle of hands rifling through the drawer's contents.

"You know," the voice said, "your pussy is very wet."

"Yes, Master," she said, gulping a bit on "Master" as she felt now cold air blowing on her slit. The breath continued, a sibilant stream up and down the length of her pussy, its coldness illuminating exactly how excited she was. The blood in her nipples beat a slow tattoo of pain that seemed to pool, collect, and transform to pleasure in her clit.

"Such a dirty little whore." The drawer clanged shut underneath her.

"Yes, Daddy," she said, her voice faltering just a tiny bit. She felt something hard pressed against her pudendum, just at the crux of her slit. Something hard and cool pressing there, waiting. She didn't recognize it, exactly.

It could be the letter opener, she thought, but then she remembered that she hadn't put it back in the desk after opening the day's mail—she remembered seeing it on the desk's surface as she was getting ready to leave, packing her magazine and her empty lunch containers in her tote bag, preparing to switch into her drive-home sneakers, looking forward to an evening of television and takeout with the boyfriend, a date for which, if her internal clock was at all correct, she was now horribly late.

She felt the metal implement slowly inch its way down her pussy, pressing with an excruciating, pleasurable precision. Slowly down her slit it moved, down, down, down the center of her cunt, pausing deliciously over her clit, passing it, descending to her cunt's opening, slipping in for a moment, drifting out, sliding with her wetness across her perineum to her asshole, and back up again. Over and over. The gliding smoothness of the unknown instrument told her how wet she was. The secretary could feel her pleasure burgeon and swell, she could almost smell her orgasm.

Which she knew, from experience, would be delayed, possibly denied, depending on the capricious malice of her dominator. Almost without her awareness, the secretary arched yet a bit more to meet the touch of the metal, now grown warm with her body heat; she willed it to linger on her clit just a moment more, just a moment, just there, just now.

"You're not going to come," the voice said, low and casual.

"No, Boss," she responded with just a hint of sadness. She knew that she wouldn't be allowed to come, she knew it with every memory of these little experiences, and yet she had hoped, perhaps, that this time it would be different. They had been meeting like this for several months now. It had started when, as a punishment for the secretary's habitual lateness, she had been summoned into her boss's office and told that she would be kept late, two minutes for every minute that she had been tardy, and that perhaps this lesson would teach her the meaning and the value of time.

It had begun with her sitting at her desk, not working, just sitting, under the boss's watchful eye. A week later, she was late again, and again the punishment and again the sitting, this time with the boss behind her, standing, and this time the boss made her sit especially upright. When the secretary's head dipped, a ruler struck—*thwack!*—loudly on the laminate beside her hand.

The next time, she had to stand, bent over on the desk. After serving her twenty-four minutes exactly, she went to the ladies' room to relieve herself; to her surprise, her panties were delicately glossed with her own egg white wetness, the soft sea pungency of her desire wafting up to her from between her parted thighs.

And so it had progressed, slowly. From sitting to standing, from standing bent over to this same bent position, ever more exposed, ever more open, supplicant and willing, a slow and slippery slope of submission that inexorably led her to this moment, the close of a day when she had been not-quite-but-almost willfully late, and her present position: kowtowing on the desk, nipples exposed and tortured, panties down, hose rent, her pussy drippy wet from the touch of an unknown office tool, and riding the knife's edge between fear and desire for what would happen next.

"Put your face on the desk, and turn your eyes to the window." She did as she was told, feeling the cool laminate under her flushed cheek and seeing that outside the large plate glass windows it was dark, the city lit up like a starlet's mirror.

"Stay there, slut," said the voice, behind her and farther away, moving perhaps into the office, perhaps down the corridor of the reception area for her boss and into the open area of the lesser, general office assistants.

"Yes, Daddy," she said.

She heard footsteps approaching her, coming around her side to the front of the desk; she felt a hand slide through her hair. Soft breath on her ear and the whispered words, "So lovely," and the feel of lips on her ear. A hand snaked under her chest, pulling gently on the painful clip and then removing it, first one and then the other.

"Your nipples are sore, aren't they?"

"Yes, Boss."

"You'd like me to kiss them, wouldn't you?"

"Yes, Boss." She gulped. Fingers tenderly rubbed her nipples, and an exquisite mix of pain and relief coursed through them, down her solar plexus and directly into her clit.

"I'm not going to." Her nipples were dropped. Footsteps

again, stopping with the boss behind her. She heard it before she felt it: a swooping cut through the air that ended in a flash of pain on her ass. Then a relentlessly gentle tapping of blows covering her behind with dull, brutal kisses. The punctuation of a thwacking blow, a pause and a delicious scrape of the letter opener's blade. The ruler rained down on her ass, her thighs, and she could feel them glow and heat, the blows causing her to inhale sharply. And then they stopped.

"Take your hands and spread your asscheeks," she heard.

"Yes, Sir," she said, slightly unsure how to respond, and fearing retribution. She did as she was told, taking her round ass in her manicured fingers and spreading it wide, aware that she was exposing the dusky rose of her anus and both shamed and excited that she was doing so.

"Very nice," she could hear her boss say, and then heard footsteps that came closer and stopped, obscuring her view of the window. Before her was her boss's waist, a belt, an expensive shirt tucked into even more expensive slacks. Broad hands holding a golf club. A driver.

"You can imagine what this is for."

"Yes, Boss."

One hand balanced the club against the desk, directly in front of the secretary's eyes. Another dipped into a pocket and withdrew a condom. The boss unwrapped the condom and slid it down over the handle of the club, retrieved a rubber band from the caddy on the desk and rubber-banded the condom in place, then picked up the club and walked back to the rear of the secretary.

The secretary felt frozen. She did not want the club in her. It looked long and menacing. Her mind raced with what the boss could do to her insides with it. She might be a tall woman, the secretary thought, but she had a rather small pussy. And her ass...she willed herself to keep her asscheeks spread apart with her hands, but she felt herself tense up, nearly to the point of shaking on the table.

A hand smoothed her lower back, rubbing gently over the cleft where her lower back swelled into her butt, tenderly cupping her asscheeks, soothing her flesh as a trainer would a trembling mare. The hand dipped between her thighs, slipped between the wet-slick folds of her labia, and knowingly rubbed her clit for a few moments.

The secretary felt her body start to relax a bit and surrender to the pleasure. The voice behind her was whispering sweet nothings, and while the secretary listened for words that she had to respond to, she heard none, and let them wash over her, causing her to relax.

"I'm going to fuck your pussy with this club."

"Yes, Master," she responded.

"You want me to, don't you, whore?"

The secretary paused. "Yes, Daddy," she admitted, as much to her boss as to herself.

The club entered her pussy, shocking and cold and hard, the boss's fingers still on her pussy. Her face on the desk, her hands spreading her asscheeks, her weight on her chest, she had a hard time pressing into the hand, but she pressed nonetheless. Despite the ungainliness of her position—or perhaps because of it—despite the fact that anyone from any office tower could see her illuminated in this position—or perhaps because of it—she felt intense pleasure rush through her. The club felt so hard that she clenched her pussy muscles around it. Once more, she could nearly smell her come, her orgasm shimmering before her, a pulsating pleasure cloud, fulsome and ready to release.

The hand stopped, the club withdrew.

"I'm going to fuck your ass now."

"No, Sir," she said, starting up, almost before she realized it. "Please. Don't."

She felt a hand on her head, she felt her hair yanked and her neck snapping back. She felt the warm breath of her boss on her cheek; she heard the voice menacing, no longer dispassionate, in her ear.

"You will get fucked in your ass," the voice said. "You want it. Tell me you want it, slut."

A pause. The secretary's breath was ragged. "No," she gasped.

The hand pulled farther back on her hair, craning her head uncomfortably. Another hand grasped a nipple between a cruel forefinger and thumb and pinched.

"You will get fucked," the voice repeated. "You want it. Tell me you want it, you dirty whore."

Another pause. A lifetime of pauses and the infinite eternal moment that stretches through the barest flicker of time. The sound of two humans breathing, ragged and taut. A palpable susurration of wills.

Her body slumped slightly. "Yes, Daddy," the secretary's voice was small and acquiescent, "I want you to fuck my ass."

She heard herself being called a good girl, she felt herself being pushed into her previous position, she felt her hands being placed onto her ass, her own fingers pressing into her buttcheeks and spreading them.

She felt something cold splatter on her ass. She felt the slow pressure of the golf club handle entering her ass, pushing slowly, inexorably, blindly past her sphincter. She felt it glide in, in, in her ass. She felt the pain.

And then she felt the glimmer of pleasure.

"So beautiful," her boss said from well behind her, standing, the secretary guessed, far enough away to watch the club penetrate her ass, watch her asshole slowly and, almost against her will, open up for it.

A hand crept between her thighs, slipping onto her clit and beginning to rub. It went on rubbing as the club entered her ass, paused at its apex and then again as it was almost all the way out of her. The secretary felt the vibrations of the club's flanged tip pass her G-spot in each movement, the pleasure-laden pain of fullness and the pleasurable near-absence.

She felt herself very close to coming, and she had to hold on not to do so. The hand on her cunt was rubbing so well and so effectively she felt her body wanting to drop, down, down into orgasm, to collapse upon itself shuddering and inexplicable there on the desk, but she dare not.

"Would you like to come?" the boss asked. The boss knew— the boss always knew when she wanted to come.

"Yes, Master," she moaned, nearly inarticulate, pleasure-pushed.

"Push down," said the boss, "push against my finger, push against the club, push down as hard as you can, whore."

"Yes, Daddy," she moaned, pushing, willing her pussy to reject the orgasm, to expel it out of her, and as she did, she felt it swell, and grow, like a tsunami, and she gushed, a slick of girl come spurting out of her, drenching the hand of her boss, and pooling on the acrylic carpet protector beneath her.

She collapsed on the desk and felt the club being gently removed from her ass. She felt the cool blade of a pair of scissors slicing off her stockings and the packing tape binding her legs to the desk. She felt hands grasping her and pulling her up off the desk, holding her, and she felt her boss's lips on her own.

"That was a good orgasm, wasn't it?" her boss asked. The secretary nodded weakly, more vulnerable now than she had been before, splayed and impaled on the desk.

"Very good," the boss said and kissed her tenderly. "Now get on your knees and thank me properly." The secretary dropped to her knees, pushed the thought of her undoubtedly pissed-off waiting boyfriend out of her mind, unzipped her boss's pants, pulled them down—her panties too—and happily buried her tongue in the other woman's wet, aching, and swollen pussy.

"Very good," the boss said, "very good work...."

RUNNING WILD

Shanna Germain

It had been a bitch of a summer. My girlfriend Tammy dumped me for the town vet, rumor had it that my husband Ken was off shoving his big haying hands up the crotch of Della Jean, the new waitress down at Marcy's Deli, and my favorite mare was about to foal, so I couldn't even take a ride to get my rocks off.

Thank God for the new horse trainer, Bobby Deline. I knew his name, but I didn't know where he came from—Ken hired him while I was still in bed over Tammy pitching me. (I told Ken it was the flu, and who was he to argue, when Della Jean's bed seemed open to him?) By the time I finally got my ass back together, Bobby'd been here working the foals for nearly a week.

I'd dragged my sorry butt out on the porch earlier, taken one look at Bobby, naked but for his blue jeans and boots, lunging the colts in big circles, and gone right back in the house. I'm not much for a whole lot of makeup—strictly natural, down-home country girl that I am—but a little shampoo in my hair and a nice pair of jeans seemed like a necessity about then.

Now, I leaned on the cut-fence rail and watched him work. He lunged the filly without a lead, making her move in circles around him with just his voice and the leather lunge whip. He handled that whip like he was born to, and I wondered if he was. Seemed to have a real knack for getting that filly to behave without even touching her with the leather. I recognized the filly right off as Mysterious Doll's newest; she's got the same high step as her mama, the same blaze of white down the center of her bay face. Not to mention her mama's stubborn temper, so I was surprised she was obeying him so well, without a single toss of her head. Some men had that power; I'd seen it a few times in my years on the barrel-racing and bronco circuits. I'd had a few even, men who knew how to tame me with nothing more than the threat of a whip. My husband wasn't one of them. But I figured it wasn't his fault; we married young, barely old enough to drink, and how are you to know anything about what you need at that age?

Bobby must have known I was there, leaning on the fence to watch him work. Protocol would say that he should take a moment to welcome the woman of the farm, the wife of the man who paid his check, but I didn't stand much by protocol and I guessed he didn't either. He sure didn't take his eyes off the filly, even though I must have willed him to about a hundred times. He concentrated on her like she was the only thing he had to worry about in his life, like all of his being was wrapped up in training her properly.

Finally, when her hindquarters were lathered up and she was breathing heavy, Bobby flicked the long black whip in front of her nose, and she came to a dead stop. I could see why Ken had hired him—my husband didn't have a clue what to do with the women in his life, but he sure knew just what his horses needed.

"Stay," Bobby said. She let her head drop to the ground and snorted into the dirt. But she stayed.

Bobby turned his attention away from the filly and started toward me. He looked as good from the front as he did from the back, strong chest muscles and a row of stomach muscles just under the skin. I gave my best smile—I've got a good smile, or so I've been told—and tilted my head. In my chest, my heart did a lopsided lope.

But as he got closer, I realized he'd fooled me. He might have turned his body away from the filly, but his attention was still on her. Don't ask me how I could tell; something in his eyes, in the way he seemed to be listening behind him. He wasn't the least bit interested in me; he was testing the filly. Would she bolt, now that he didn't have his eyes on her? Or would she behave for him?

He stopped in front of me, close enough that I could see the dark hairs spiraling up his flat belly, the drops of sweat caught there. He still didn't acknowledge me, but I knew that he was aware of my movements, just as he was aware of the filly's behind him. I felt like it was me being tested; my palms were sweaty against the fence and I wanted to adjust my jeans, which suddenly felt too tight at the crotch. Instead, I watched his hand, the easy way he held the whip's length coiled.

We waited, the three of us, not moving. Just the lazy switch of the filly's tail, the tilt of her head as she watched him. I knew how she felt; should she do what she could get away with? Or should she continue to obey his spoken command? If she was anything like her mama, I doubted even Bobby could tame her completely.

Just as the filly lifted her front hoof off the ground, barely an inch, just to test the waters, Bobby turned around. Before I think she even realized she was going to disobey his command,

Bobby was at her head, praising her. I watched as he pulled half a carrot from his pocket and let her lip it off his palm.

"Follow," he said, and damned if that filly didn't prick up her ears at his voice, and then follow him like she'd been a pack-horse for twenty years.

"Well-behaved filly you've got there, ma'am," he said as he went by. He looked me up and down as he passed. One side of his grin was higher than the other. It turned his face from thoughtfully rugged to mischievous. It said "follow" without saying anything at all. It made me wish I had ears to prick up.

I watched the two of them walk away, the filly's curvy rear end and his muscular one. Damn. Maybe this summer wouldn't turn out to be so bad after all.

I gave Bobby time to get the filly cooled and settled in her stall before I went and found him.

He was in the tack room, smoothing saddle soap on a bridle. I leaned against the doorjamb and took in his smooth bare chest, the biceps that bobbed as he worked the leather. I had dreams of him cross-tying me like a wild mare, of pressing that leather to my skin.

"You must be the lady of the barn," he said without looking up.

I liked that, that he either didn't assume I was the lady of the house, or that he knew something about me.

"I must be," I said.

"Saw you riding the barrels in Sisters last year," he said.

"Yeah, what'd you think?"

He looked up, crooked grin a little higher. "Thought you could have given up some control, trust your mare a little more. She would have gone faster 'round that second barrel."

I didn't say anything. I'd finished second in that run, just behind the top rider in the state.

He hung the bridle up and wiped his hands on a rag.

"And I think you're not standing there just to ask me what I think about your riding."

I cocked my head. "Really? Why am I standing here?"

With his easy stride, he was at my head in a second. He put the flat of his hand against my cheek.

"Because you've been running wild all summer long, and you need someone to put some reins on you and put you in check."

I tried to think, but his hand moved down, grasped the back of my head and held me in place.

"Who told you that?" I asked, once I could think again.

"Your husband," he said.

I laughed. "Right." Like he cared.

Bobby moved my head forward until his lips pressed against mine. He didn't kiss me; he talked to me, moving his lips so I could feel every word like some kind of Braille.

"He didn't hire me to break your horses," Bobby said. "He hired me to break you. I've been waiting all week for you to get your ass out of bed and show up."

I didn't believe him, but it didn't matter. His hands had captured the back of my head and his lips had captured the front. His tongue worked its way into my mouth, as persistent and hard as a bit. I welcomed it, the way it felt against my teeth, the flavor of him, slightly metallic, laced with dried hay and tobacco. As his tongue worked, so did his hands, pulling me against him. The hard bulge of his cock pressed into the hot spot in my jeans. I aimed my hips, got the length of it pressed to just the right spot. I wanted to ride him, to feel his muscles move beneath me. I reached for him, to put my hands on his hips and pull him even closer, but he caught my wrists with one hand.

He pulled one of the leather whips off a hook and I thought—hoped—he might bind my wrists with it. But he just held it, the way he'd held the whip when he was working with the filly.

"Now," he said. "Let's try that again. Turn around. Hands against the wall."

Without the lead, he'd been powerful. With that piece of leather in his hand, it moved him beyond power somehow. There was nothing to do but obey. I turned and pressed my palms to the rough wood.

He kicked my legs apart. Then he reached around and unsnapped my jeans with one hand. His chest pressed against my back, and I could smell the leather and oil that came off his skin. His fingers worked inside my panties, opened my lips.

"See?" he said as his fingers worked. "You're so wet. You already know how to obey, don't you? You've just forgotten?"

I couldn't answer. All I could do was feel his fingers on me, in me. My head rolled back to rest against him. Ah, God. How long had it been?

I was so close, so close. I wanted... I moved my hips to press harder against his fingers.

The snap of the leather stung a little, but that pain was nothing compared to the way he took his hand out of my underwear and wiped his fingers on my jeans. My clit throbbed, aching to be finished. My hard breathing was the only sound in the room.

Still behind me, Bobby took my hands off the wall and pulled my arms behind me. He wrapped the leather around my wrists, and then looped it around my waist. It was like being calf-roped standing up. I'd wanted it earlier, but now I wanted just to stroke myself, to feel the relief of finally coming.

"I didn't want to tie you," Bobby said in my ear. His voice gave me shivers. "But I don't want you using those hands to get yourself off," he said, as though he could read my mind.

He turned me around to face him.

"Follow," he said.

Something in me resisted, but the power of his voice, the way he walked away from me as though he knew I would trail after him, made it so I couldn't say no. I followed him out into the barn, followed him down the cement walkway, the horses watching from their stalls. He stopped at a clean, empty stall at the end. The Dutch door was closed at the top half and open at the bottom.

Bobby gestured at the door.

He didn't really expect me to bow through that, did he? His look told me that he did. Shit. My jeans were still undone, and I wasn't sure what my balance would be like. Still, I wanted it. That was the truth of it. I wanted someone to tell me how to behave. Wanted someone to tell me to crawl. Still, I couldn't do it.

"Please," I said.

Bobby stepped up to me. I couldn't do anything but watch as he pulled the two halves of my shirt apart. Good thing it was old, and the buttonholes were loose, or he would have ripped the buttons off. As it was, the buttons slid right out of their trappings. Bobby didn't even look at the lacy bra I'd put on, he merely popped the front open with two fingers to expose my breasts.

"I always thought we put too many trappings on," he said as his fingers pinched the tender ends of my nipples. "Horses and women."

My clit might have been sleeping, waiting, but when he touched me, it woke back up. Howled at me, even.

Bobby pulled my nipples downward. Pain and pleasure exploded in my chest. I twisted my shoulders, trying to get out, to lessen the pain, but with my hands tied, it was impossible. I was making small mews, like a lost animal.

He didn't stop. He tugged my nipples toward the cement

floor until my body had no choice but to follow, until I was on my knees, just like he'd wanted me in the first place.

Even then, it wasn't good enough. He clucked his tongue. "I would have thought you'd be faster," he said. "But maybe you've been running wild too long. Now follow."

My nipples stretched as he pulled me toward the stall. The burn slid down from my chest, became a fire that ignited between my legs. I moved forward on my knees, following Bobby, following my own desire. I barely felt my knees against the cement. My clit took precedence over everything, begging to be touched.

He bent forward, giving my nipples a second of relief, and then he slid under the door into the stall. I followed as fast as I could, held up only by Bobby's fingers on my nipples and my own need. Once I got into the stall, Bobby let go of me. My nipples throbbed with pain when the cold air hit them. My teeth chattered. I'd never wanted to be fucked, to be ridden, so badly in my life.

"Please," I begged.

Bobby gave me that lopsided grin again.

"Please, what?"

"Please..." My teeth wouldn't stop knocking together. "Please fuck me. I want to come."

"Oh, I don't think so," Bobby said. "You're nowhere near ready for that. You need to learn the basics first."

Bobby ran his fingers, feather soft, across my chest, against the hot pink skin of my nipples. I shivered. Somewhere else in the barn, a horse whinnied. Then another. A second later, I heard Ken's tires against the gravel drive.

I opened my eyes wide at Bobby, but I couldn't speak.

He put his hand to my face. The touch was as gentle this time as it had been hard before.

"I told you earlier," he said. "Your husband didn't hire me for the horses."

He turned his back on me and moved away. When he got to the stall door, he stopped, but didn't look back.

"Stay," he said.

I closed my eyes and shook my head. But I stayed. I stayed.

PINK IS
THE ENEMY

Jocelyn Bringas

T ake off your skirt."

My fingers immediately obeyed his request and tugged the material down to the floor. I was now one thong away from being completely naked as I stood with my back facing Duke.

"What the fuck?"

I heard him get up from his chair and stomp his way to me. My heart was racing. He never got up from his chair unless something was terribly wrong. I gasped when his hands viciously grabbed my asscheeks and spread them far apart.

"Why are you wearing a pink thong?"

Crap! I had forgotten to change my underwear before coming to his home. My boss had kept me late at work and by the time I was on the freeway, there was no time to go to my apartment for an underwear change. Duke always wanted me to be at his home on time. If I was even just one second late he wouldn't bother answering the door.

My heart felt heavy knowing I had disappointed him. I had

always been so good about changing my underwear. I aimed to please him and breaking my streak made me feel really bad.

He walked away, leaving me standing there frozen. I didn't want to move an inch. Last time I moved to look for him I was put in detention. His form of detention was no touching and no fucking for two days. Not having his cock for forty-eight hours had been pure torture and I didn't want to risk experiencing that again.

I wondered if he was going to punish me for my mistake. I did deserve to be punished. Maybe this little error would work out in my favor? My mind raced with all the different possibilities. Was he searching his home for a new toy to use?

It couldn't be the riding crop; he'd used that last night. He never used the same toy twice in a row. Perhaps it was the rabbit vibrator? He loved to fuck my pussy while he jammed it up my ass.

I glanced over at the ticking antique grandfather clock standing against the wall. He loved collecting different types of clocks. It was exactly eleven p.m. I thought he'd only be gone for five minutes at the most.

At two minutes past twelve, I heard the familiar stomping of his footsteps on the stairs. He pressed his cool body against my back. My whole body shivered from the sudden skin to skin contact. His stiff cock was comfortably nestled in the crack of my ass. I started to breathe heavier when a cold object slid up the side of my right thigh. I assumed it was a new toy but I heard a snip.

With my peripheral vision, I looked down and saw he was holding a pair of shiny silver scissors. He had cut the fabric to one side of my pink thong and now he did the same to the other. A loud clank echoed off the walls as he tossed the scissors onto the wood floor. The thong was still hanging off me, my closed legs keeping it from falling. Slowly, he pulled the thong away from my body, causing it to rub against my aching pussy.

"Turn around."

With the tips of his fingers, he held on to the pink thong like it was a piece of filthy trash.

"You know I hate the color pink. Pink clothing is for incompetent little girls. I've told you repeatedly to never wear it."

Pink was such a wonderful color. I wished he'd understand that but I knew he wouldn't. I flinched when he suddenly squished my thong into a ball.

"Open wide."

Once I opened my mouth, he stuffed the thong inside. My mouth instantly watered upon tasting my pussy juice. He walked back to his chair and sat down. His hard cock looked so delicious resting against his stomach.

Whenever he was sitting on his chair, he always looked like a king on his throne. I felt like a servant girl awaiting his next command.

"You really love to wear pink, don't you?"

I nodded my head up and down. He rolled his eyes at my response.

"The only pink you can wear is the pinkness from me spanking you."

With his finger, he beckoned me to approach him. He reached underneath his chair and retrieved a wooden spanking paddle. Despite my expressionless face, I was smiling inside. The wooden spanking paddle was one of my favorite toys.

"Turn around and stick your ass high up in the air."

I immediately assumed the position, my pussy already tingling with anticipation. The first strike had enough power to trigger an earthquake in California. Each strike he made got progressively harder and came faster. My clit was pulsating madly, itching to be rubbed.

When he was done, he threw the paddle onto the floor. There was a brief silence and I eagerly awaited his next move. The click of a Polaroid camera broke the silence. He wasn't into digital cameras because he found them to be such a hassle. I heard him shake the picture dry.

"Come here and sit on my lap."

My ass was on fire and once it touched his cold skin, I winced. He showed me the picture and I was amazed at how pink my ass looked. That kind of pink was way better than the pink thong.

"Spit the thong out."

The wet thong landed on the floor. It looked like the life had been sucked away from it.

"If I ever see you wear any pink again, you will regret it and you may have to live without my cock for some time. Understand that?"

I gulped. We'd been fucking for over two years and the thought of living without his delicious cock frightened me. I nodded my head in agreement. His hands gripped my hot pink ass and he pulled me down so that I was sitting on his cock. Reaching around me, he spread my pussy lips apart and jammed his cock inside.

Relaxing against his chest, I enjoyed the ride.

When I arrived at my apartment the next day, I didn't waste any time. I immediately plucked every single piece of pink clothing and underwear I had out of my bedroom. I learned my lesson about the color pink. It was a beautiful color but I could live without it. Duke was much more important to me than a silly color.

All the pink clothing I had went into a garbage bag and I drove to the nearest Goodwill donation station. Not only was I doing a favor for Duke, I was also helping the less fortunate people.

Living without Duke in my life just seemed so unbearable—I would die without him. My heart grew heavy as the image of his disappointed look flashed in my mind. I never wanted to see him look at me like that again.

This outing also gave me an opportunity to do some shopping. I stopped by Pleasure Palace, a local lingerie shop, and bought fifteen black thongs to replace the fifteen pink thongs that were now gone.

While I was in the shop, I decided to peruse the different clothing. There was a gorgeous black corset calling my name. I tried it on and adored the way it hugged my curves.

I couldn't wait to show it off to Duke and see his reaction.

"You look so fucking good."

My cheeks grew warm at his compliment. He was sitting on his chair slowly stroking his cock as he examined me with his eyes. I felt proud of myself for picking a good enough outfit for him. I was wearing my new corset, a red miniskirt, and a black thong.

"Lie down on the floor and spread your legs."

I shivered the moment the cold floor hit my back. My skirt hiked up above my hips as my legs split apart. From his chair, he leaned forward, picked up my right foot and held it up high in the air.

"No pink thong. Good job."

Duke smiled, and seeing his positive reaction made me feel fuzzy in my stomach. He pressed his lips to my toes and it took all my strength to keep from giggling. He didn't like it when I giggled because he thought only immature teenage girls did that. I sighed contentedly when his tongue traced along them.

He looked absolutely handsome sucking on my toes. I loved the way his soft blond hair fell into his eyes. All of my toes now were stuffed into his mouth as his tongue devoured them. The whole time his eyes were looking into mine.

His lips then traveled to the side of my ankle where there were some tattoos he had instructed me to get a few months ago. They were Chinese symbols for devotion and dedication. He chose those two words because he wanted a constant reminder that I was completely devoted and dedicated to him. When he was finished, he let go of my foot.

"People who are good get rewards, right?"

I nodded in agreement. He took his cock in his hand and began stroking it nonchalantly. My mouth watered as my eyes stared at his movements. With his free hand, he pointed to his hard cock and I moved to kneel before him.

The wet tip of his cock looked shiny from the light. He trailed it along my forehead and then down the side of my cheek. Once he reached my mouth, it was already open and ready for business. I sucked him as if his cock was my only source of life.

I took a deep breath through my nose, trying not to gag as he grabbed my head and began shoving himself into my mouth. Glancing upward, I saw that he had his head thrown back in pleasure as he rocked his hips back and forth.

Pulling out, he let his cock rebound against his stomach. It pointed up in the air, completely covered with my saliva.

"Suck my balls."

Sticking my tongue out, I dabbled it onto his churning balls. Then I gently grazed my teeth against them and finally sucked them into my mouth. Duke was groaning like a madman now so I intensified my suction. Within seconds, a stream of his come leaked down the side of my cheek. He quickly grabbed his cock and proceeded to empty the rest of his delicious liquid onto my face.

When he was finished, he dragged one of his fingers down

my cheek, scraping some come off. He then rubbed it onto my lips like it was lip-gloss.

"Stand up."

Once I was on my feet, he smashed his lips to mine. Our lips glided together as we engaged in a passionate kiss. The part of the corset covering my breasts had lowered so now my nipples were rubbing against his bare chest. His hands wandered down to my ass, gripping my cheeks roughly.

"Get on all fours."

My pussy was already wet and craving his cock when I got into position. His fingers tugged my thong down my thighs. I could feel his breath brushing my skin, giving me goose bumps.

I loved getting fucked from behind. There was something about being bent over and on my knees with his cock driving into me. He had complete control over all my pleasure and I was very dependent on everything he did.

My nipples grazed the floor as he slammed his cock inside my pussy. No other man has taken me to the places Duke has during sex. He knew he had power over me and used it to his advantage. I would do anything to keep him in my life.

"Say my name." Duke was close now as he panted his words out. His fingers dug deeply into my hips, his pace changing. As if to torture me, he slowed down; every few seconds he'd pull out, then shove it back in.

"Duke," I moaned and he slammed his cock all the way inside.

"Louder."

"Duke!" I shouted and he slammed into me so hard I collided with the floor.

"Fuck."

I lay flat on the floor as he started to buck his hips roughly against my ass. The beautiful sounds of our skin crashing together echoed throughout the room. With each thrust he made, the delicious pleasure started to build up.

The sensation of his cock brushing my walls got overwhelming. I started to moan louder and within seconds my pussy walls fluttered as my orgasm suddenly shook my body. Behind me, Duke growled like an animal as he held himself steady. Soon his come came pouring out, mixing with my juices. He collapsed onto my back, his sweaty chest pressing against me.

"Who do you belong to?"

"I belong to you, Duke."

"Tell me which color is the enemy."

"Pink is the enemy."

Our bodies finally separated and I turned around to face Duke. I could see the satisfaction in his blue eyes and it lifted my spirits. We engaged in a passionate kiss then, and eventually we fucked many more times that night.

SITTING ON ICE CREAM

Lisette Ashton

22:45

"You've got something on your skirt."

"Where?" Kay glanced back over her shoulder, trying to see where Jane was pointing. "On my bum?"

"Yes. A big white splotch."

Kay turned her face away so Jane couldn't see her knowing smile or the satisfied blush on her cheeks. "Of course. Now I remember. I think I was sitting on ice cream."

19:05

It was probably the crummiest chore she was expected to endure. While she loved the atmosphere of working in a theater, Kay loathed the cleaning duties that fell to her before her work properly began. She supposed, because it was a small theater, and because the management was trying to keep costs down, it was only fair that she had to do some of the menial tasks. After a matinee, and before the evening show, the theater

needed a cursory clean through. And while she accepted most of
the chores, she didn't enjoy bending over the velour chairs and
scrubbing melted ice cream out of the plush seats.

"Shouldn't you be in uniform?"

She stiffened when she heard Ted's voice: rich, powerful,
syrupy, and yet commanding. He had a way of speaking that
always sent a warm shiver coursing through the crotch of her
panties. If he had decided to go into doing voice-overs for radio
commercials, Kay thought she would buy anything he was trying to sell.

"I should be in my uniform," she admitted, not looking up,
not daring to turn and meet his gaze or his disapproving frown.
"But this chair was dirty and I wanted to..."

"Are you making excuses?"

Kay fell instantly silent.

The thrill of working in the theater was tremendous. She
got to see snatches of visiting shows. There was also the pres-
tige of being involved, even if only in a small way, with the
entertainment industry. But, more exciting than either of those
two elements: Kay got to wear a uniform. Her usherette outfit
consisted of heels, stockings, a skirt and blouse in the style of
a French maid's costume, and all of it was set off with a white
lace cap. It was one of the most arousing ensembles she had ever
had to wear. The stockings hugged her thighs and calves. Hold-
ups, they bit snugly against the tops of her inner thighs. The
high hem of the skirt, and the low neckline of the blouse, were
like a conspiracy to make her indecent. The ordeal of having to
wear such revealing clothes was a sheer delight to the reluctant
exhibitionist that lurked in the shadows of her psyche.

And she was getting paid for the privilege!

However—even more exciting, and possibly the most ap-
pealing part of the whole experience—she was in a role where

she had to take orders from the incredibly authoritative Ted.

"All cleaning duties should be finished by nineteen hundred hours," Ted reminded her. He spoke as though he was reading her duties from a memorized manual. His voice had the toneless inflection of someone with a strong military heritage.

"I know, but…"

"By nineteen oh five all female staff should have reported to the changing rooms and be in full uniform, ready for inspection."

"I know but…"

She wanted to tell him he was being sanctimonious. She wanted to remind him that the phrase "all female staff" referred only to her and her fellow usherette Jane—who was late again this evening. It was a small theater yet Ted made it sound like a platoon of usherettes was conscripted every night. She longed to say something that would usurp his pompous attitude. But she couldn't bring herself to challenge his authority.

"I know I should have…" she began.

"It's now nineteen oh five, Kay," Ted broke in. "It's nineteen oh five and you're not in full uniform. Can you please tell me why you've broken the rules?"

Kay couldn't say a word.

The truth was that she had been working hard, trying to make sure Ted's theater was presentable for the evening customers when they arrived. Trying to please him with her attention to detail. Kay knew that she was supposed to be in uniform by this point. But she also knew she would never be able to explain as much to Ted. Nervousness and the thrill of being the object of his wrath kept her silent.

"You've been disobedient again, haven't you, Kay?"

She finally turned to face him, nodding.

"This is the third time you've broken the rules, isn't it?"

Again she responded with a single nod. Her gaze was lowered, her eyes fixed on the polished shine of Ted's boots against the meticulous expanse of the theater carpet.

"You've been working here a month and I haven't yet reprimanded you, have I, Kay?"

She shook her head. "No, Sir."

Ted sighed. The sound registered somewhere between frustration and smug satisfaction. "Go into the changing room," he snapped. "Change into your uniform. Then wait in my office. I shall be along to reprimand you shortly."

Trembling, and adamant he wouldn't see how he had affected her, Kay grabbed her cleaning things and rushed to do as he had commanded. "Yes, Sir," she whispered, hurrying past his side.

He carried the musky fragrance of an Armani perfume.

Expensive.

Potent.

Exciting.

She noticed the scent as she brushed past his manly frame. And then she was running down the theater's aisle and bustling to the backstage area allotted to the front of house staff.

19:55

Of course, he wasn't going to spank her.

She knew that wasn't going to happen because spankings only happened in the books she read. And in those delicious dark fantasies that kept her awake at night as she plunged her fingers against the yielding flesh of her sex. Spanking happened quite a lot at those times. And it was always hard, merciless, punishing and fantastic. Sometimes it was being done with a paddle. Other times it was the spiky bristles of a hairbrush. From private (and sadly solitary) experiments she knew that both implements produced their own distinctive responses. But most times, when the fantasies were at their most powerful, Kay was being spanked by an open bare hand.

Ted's hand.

She quivered against the leather stool in front of his desk. Her uniform of short skirt and stockings allowed the tops of her thighs to be kissed by the leather seat. It was warm against her skin and made her think of lovers nestling against her buttocks. If she hadn't been wearing panties, she felt sure she would have left a small puddle of moisture in the center of the seat. Her heart pounded solidly and her breath came in long, asthmatic gasps.

When the door behind her opened, Kay's heartbeat quickened.

Perspiration glistened on her brow.

The heat between her thighs grew more ferocious.

"Front of house opens at twenty hundred hours," Ted announced.

First she caught the scent of his Armani cologne.

Then he stepped into view.

Because she was sitting down, he seemed larger.

Stronger.

More potent and powerful than in her wildest and wettest fantasies. His jaw was strong and determined. His eyes were hard, unfathomable flints. He looked groomed and tailored to perfection and she didn't think there had ever been a man she found more desirable and masterful.

"I don't have time to take care of your discipline now," Ted said stiffly. "But I shall want to see you back here after the intermission."

He paused for a moment and she could almost see the calculations being made behind his frown. The doors opened at

20:00. Curtain up was scheduled for 20:30. This evening's show, a heavily touted performance of some amateur musical, was meant to begin its intermission at 21:15. After a fifteen minute break the show would resume for its final half at 21:30.

"I want you back here straight after the intermission. If you arrive any later than twenty-one thirty-five the punishment will be severe."

She swallowed and dragged her gaze up to meet his face. He hadn't bothered sitting behind his desk.

He simply stood by her side.

Towering over her.

Glowering down.

"Punishment?"

A cruel smile cracked his frown. "You've been a very naughty girl, Kay," he muttered. "I need to show you what happens to very naughty girls under my command."

Her blush was hot enough to sear her cheeks. Deciding that she had been dismissed until their dreaded (desired) appointment at 21:35, Kay slid out of her chair and started for the door.

"Before you go..."

She paused with her hand on the doorknob. It was large, round and thick against her fingers. She only had to twist it once and she would open up his office and break the enchanting spell that came from being alone with Ted and his glorious disapproval. Sliding her fingers away, turning slowly to face him, she lowered her gaze again.

"Yes, Sir?"

"Before you go, I'd like your panties, please. You may leave them on my desk and then return to your duties."

"You want my..."

He didn't let her finish the question.

"AY ESS AY PEE, Kay. The doors open in a moment and Jane can't handle the entire theater on her own."

Despite his insistent tone, she hesitated.

Clearly Jane had arrived (late again) but Kay didn't bother processing that unimportant detail. She was still bowled over by the fact that Ted had demanded her panties. His casual instruction, so similar to those she had enjoyed in her lonely fantasy sessions, was enough to make her wonder if she had properly heard his words or only imagined them.

"You want my *panties*?"

"On the desk. Now."

Her hand trembled as she reached beneath the hem of her skirt. She awkwardly fumbled to find the waistband, and then tugged them until they started to come down. The crotch kissed a sticky farewell to her labia. And then she was treated to the sensation of the cool office air teasing her pussy lips. Blushing madly, deafened by the pounding of her heartbeat, she drew the panties down her thighs and let them fall to her ankles. Stepping daintily out of the white cotton knickers, she bent down and picked them up. Trying not to meet Ted's gaze, she walked back to his desk and placed the panties in the center.

"Thank you." There was the faintest trace of a smile in his voice. "Now hurry along. And don't be late for our twenty-one thirty-five."

20:35

The minutes crept past in a torturous meandering rush.

Kay greeted and seated the modest lines of sedately dressed patrons. She noticed Jane, on the opposite side of the auditorium, and wished they had a moment where they could chat. Jane wasn't exactly a friend. But she had worked at the theater longer than Kay and would know more about Ted and his unexpected behavior. Kay wanted to know if the punishment he had planned for her was something he doled out to every member of staff. Or if he was making an exception for her because he could see she was aroused by his masterful authority.

But brooding on the question didn't help. Jane was too busy to talk. And, even if there had been an opportunity to exchange a few words, Kay couldn't think of a way to tactfully broach the subject. Worse still: she was acutely conscious of the fact that she wasn't wearing panties.

The air in the theater had never before felt cold.

Yet now it was an icy caress that constantly teased her sex.

She suspected the heat of her arousal was causing a marked contrast. But dwelling on that notion only made her remember why she wasn't wearing any panties. Similarly, each time she contemplated how Ted planned to punish her, Kay was almost crippled by the wet flood of anticipation. When the houselights finally dimmed she collapsed into one of the seats in the back row and pressed the heel of her hand against her groin.

The desire to climax, and exorcise her body's need for satisfaction, was strong. But she suspected that if Ted discovered her masturbating in the rear stalls, whatever punishment he had planned would be far more severe.

That thought alone was enough to bring her close to the point of climax. Squirming against the velour seats, aware her bare buttocks were being stroked by the warm weave of the fabric, Kay closed her eyes and struggled to stave off the rush of satisfaction.

21:35

The opening of the show had sped past in a dull haze. Kay vaguely noted that the actors brought new meaning to the word *amateur* in the phrase *amateur production*. But her thoughts were preoccupied with more important matters than critical commentary. She went through the routine of selling ice cream and soft drinks in the intermission, aware that the clock was constantly creeping closer to her 21:35 appointment with Ted. Her bowels churned with a combination of dread and desire. The thrill of not knowing what would happen was as maddening as each of the potential scenarios she envisaged. Several times she found herself asking customers to repeat themselves as she realized her distracted thoughts had dominated her consciousness. And, all the time, she was thinking of what Ted would do to her once she was alone in his office. Eventually, as the clock neared 21:30, she decided the ordeal was more than she wanted to suffer. When she got to his office she was going to tell him that he couldn't treat his staff with sexual harassment of this magnitude. And, once the decision was made, she was determined to stand by it.

"Twenty-one thirty-five," Ted said, stepping into the room and pausing behind her.

Kay heard the sound of the door closing.

The twist of a key turning in the lock.

The whisper of blinds being drawn.

"I'm glad to see there are some circumstances where you can be punctual."

His words were enough to make her rethink her plans to accuse him of sexual harassment. As soon as he spoke she recanted her thoughts of refusing his commands. Whatever he wanted from her, however he wanted to proceed with her punishment, Kay was willing to suffer every arduous moment.

"Stand up."

She stood.

"Bend over the desk."

She bent.

Her backside was raised high. The short hem of the skirt lifted as she leant forward. Without glancing back over her shoulder Kay knew that the secrets of her sex were already exposed to him. A shiver of delicious arousal sailed through her body. Because she had spent the last two hours in a state of borderline climax it was almost enough to make her shriek with orgasm.

"You've been a very naughty girl, Kay. Haven't you?"

"Yes, Sir."

Fingers stroked against her bare buttocks.

The torment was excruciating.

Kay yearned to feel the hard slap of Ted's strong hand against her rear. She was on the verge of begging for him to slam his palm swiftly against her cheek. The need was so strong she could almost hear the sound of bare flesh breaking sharp against bare flesh, feel the warm sting of one bruised cheek, savor the insidious warmth as it spread to her sex.

His fingers continued to tease and appraise her backside. She was aware of his caresses shifting from the snug elastic at the tops of her stockings. Then trailing gently over her raised cheeks. Then sliding daringly close to the split of her sex.

A shiver rippled through her. The inner muscles of her sex clenched and convulsed with greedy approbation.

"I could go easy on you," Ted murmured. "I could let your earlier transgression slide. I could be lenient and tell you to stand up and get back to your duties."

She knew he could do all of those things. But the idea that he might made her want to scream for him not to show leniency.

She was aroused.

Exposed.

And stretched across his desk.

Her desire to suffer his punishment bordered on desperation. Trembling against the desk, she wondered if there was any way she dared to make him know how badly she wanted to suffer his discipline.

"But I never show leniency," Ted muttered.

Kay released a soft sigh of gratitude.

And then felt his first glorious strike.

Her buttocks were held high. The weight of the desk supported her stomach. And she was pushed against it as his hand slapped hard against her rear. The sting of pain was sudden, sharp and blissfully sweet. She snatched a breath, savoring the bright warmth of where his hand had landed. And then he was slapping another blow against her backside. The sound was crisp. Deafening. The heat was enormous. And when she cried out in response, her reactions had nothing to do with pain or discomfort. Her moan came from the growing swell of euphoria that threatened to tear through her loins.

"You understand this punishment is necessary, don't you?"

"Yes, Sir."

She spat the words between clenched teeth. If she opened her mouth fully Kay knew she was going to shriek. His hand repeatedly slapped hard against her backside. The sting of warmth quickly inspired a volcanic heat. Her buttocks reddened beneath the blows and her sex smoldered with growing need.

In the guileless attempts she had made to spank herself, Kay had never known such an extreme reaction. When she had secretly imagined Ted administering this style of punishment, she had always known he would be masterful. But she had never thought he could be this commanding.

"You understand I need to inflict discipline to ensure the smooth running of the theater, don't you?"

She paused before answering, knowing he was about slap another crisp blow against her sex. She could picture the lips of her pussy: wet and gaping for him. She could imagine the pale pink skin was flushed to a glistening fuchsia with the force of her arousal. The cheeks of her bottom would be blushing and swollen. And she knew that her body had never been so humiliatingly exposed to any man ever before. When the slap landed, she stiffened and again resisted the urge to release her orgasm.

"Yes, Sir," she gasped. "I understand."

She continued to clench her teeth together as Ted delivered two more blows. He paused from the punishment and drew a deep breath.

"Do you also understand that this is exciting me?"

She glanced behind herself and moaned.

The front panel of his immaculate pants was distorted by a large bulge. The knowledge that she had fueled his arousal, and that she was in the perfect position to take advantage of his excitement, made the inner muscles of her sex convulse with a fresh and greedy need.

She reached out awkwardly for him.

His zipper came down in an instant.

The clean, throbbing length of his erection pushed out from the gaping mouth of the fly. Not bothering to consider whether the action might meet with his approval or not, Kay encircled his shaft with one hand and drew him close to the heated slit of her pussy.

Ted gripped her waist and pushed his shaft inside.

They groaned together.

Kay didn't know how she had resisted her climax for so long. But when Ted's length plunged into her, she released the howl of satisfaction that her body had needed. As he pushed himself in as deep as he could, the coarse weave of his pants scratched her sore buttocks.

But that reminder of her discomfort only added to her thrill.

Thrusting her backside to meet him, determined to devour as much of his length as her sex could accept, Kay rode herself up and down him as her body was buffeted by one orgasm after another.

Ted finally pulled himself from her.

His shaft had erupted with a forceful thrust that left her slick with his ejaculate. Delicately, almost tenderly, he helped her from the desk and told her that her punishment for the evening was now concluded.

Kay tried to compose herself as she stood on trembling legs.

She felt used, disheveled and deliciously satisfied. Studying him from beneath lowered lids, she glanced at the desk. "May I have my panties back?"

Ted shook his head. "I'll keep them here."

"But..."

The slick fluid of his semen still filled her. She was breathless from satisfaction and already eager to suffer his discipline again. But she could see he would not tolerate insubordination. The tone of his voice suggested a repeated request would meet with a flat and uncompromising refusal. Nevertheless, she continued to try and think of a way to retrieve the panties.

"But..."

"But?" he repeated.

His tone was half-mocking. His eyes glinted mischievously. Kay wanted to tell him that she needed the panties, and that they would protect her uniform skirt when his seed eventually began to leak from her.

Ted grinned as though he had read her thoughts. Tucking his spent length back into his pants, instantaneously resuming an air of perfectly groomed authority, he said, "If anyone asks about the wet stain on your skirt, just tell them you accidentally sat on some ice cream."

22:45

In the changing room, getting ready to step out of her uniform and get back into her regular clothes, Kay realized Jane was standing behind her. She turned and smiled at her fellow usherette. "I haven't had a chance to say hi to you this evening."

"It's been a hectic night, hasn't it?" Jane said, rolling her eyes. "Ted wasn't happy about me being late again," she explained. She looked set to say more and then pointed at Kay's backside. "You've got something on your skirt."

"Where?" Kay glanced back over her shoulder, trying to see where Jane was pointing. "On my bum?"

"Yes. A big white splotch."

Kay turned her face away so Jane couldn't see her knowing smile or the satisfied blush on her cheeks. "Of course. Now I remember. I think I was sitting on ice cream."

Jane laughed. "Isn't that a coincidence?" She turned her back and showed the rear of her skirt to Kay. A spreading white stain flourished from the center of the back panel. "Can you see?" Jane giggled. "Exactly the same thing's happened to me. I think I was sitting on some just before the intermission."

Kay could see.

She grinned.

It didn't trouble her that Ted administered his punishment to every member of his staff. It only made her adamant that tomorrow evening, she would spend a very long time cleaning the auditorium's seats. And she would do that every night from now on, regardless of how angry it might make Ted.

UNDER HIS HAND, I BLOSSOM

Nikki Magennis

My room is as silent as a theater before the play starts. Sun slants through the tall windows, sliced into stripes by the blinds, and falls on the pale polished floors. Dust motes dance in the lit spots. I've furnished it in exactly the style I prefer—white walls, blue and white sheets on the bed, dark stained furniture, like a Moroccan hotel. It's my sanctuary—everything arranged according to my wishes, nothing out of place. Which makes the man standing by the door all the more disturbing.

He's come straight from the office. Still in his shirt and belted trousers, with the thick watch on his wrist and the scent of work about him. Ink and telephones and signatures—he's filled with the rushing importance of his day.

I am curled on the counterpane in my bathrobe.

I wait as he circles, unclipping cuff links, rolling up his sleeves to show me those startlingly tanned arms, his burnished skin and the rough hair that is so animal-like where it crawls from underneath his cotton shirt.

I have my ankles on display, and a triangle of very pale flesh at my throat. My eyes are wide open and my mouth is a rocking bowl of a smile. My breasts are covered and I am suitably modest. No cleavage, none of the obvious seduction equipment. Lace and frills and stockings show too much artifice, and I must be a blank canvas for him to write on. I know the game and how we play it. We worked out the script months before we ever actually did anything. Every scene reminds me of our long courtship, our dangerous conversations.

"So you're into games?"
"Depends who's playing."
"What kind of games?"
"Just one."
"Will I like it?"
"We'll see."

In silence, I lie swaddled in white like a pasha. Under the bathrobe, I'm pink and damp from the shower. Smelling of rose geranium, shaved slick and smooth. Sodden with cream. This is the beginning. I must not rush. I play innocent, lying here, stretched out like a sacrifice on the flat, open altar of the bed.

He throws a look my way; a narrow look. Those eyes that judge and consider settle on me. I squirm under the weight of his gaze, wanting to unfurl like a flower hit by the sun. His mouth is a carved arabesque. He doesn't smile, his lips don't even twitch. I am placid. I let him imagine.

He approaches, and I look up to him standing over me with his hands in his pockets. He's close enough to reach out and pluck what he wishes. If I let the robe fall open, he would see the tender parts of me—breast, throat, belly, inner thighs. The platter that is my sex arranged so perfectly for him, pink lipped and plump and ready for his touch. I stay wrapped. I'm aching to be touched, but I've learned patience since I first met him. He taught me my lessons well. I remember them word for word:

"You can't rush into something like this."
"I know what I want."
"But you don't know me. You don't know if you can trust me yet."
"So when will we start?"
"When you stop asking questions."

With his movements so slow he must be thinking of something else, he unbuckles his belt. I watch and it stirs deep-seated memories.

His belt is how I first knew, the clue that gave away the secret.

The first afternoon we fucked it was full-blooded vanilla sex, merry and gasping. Afterward we lay in a mess of stripped and crumpled clothes, buttons and zips digging into my skin and leaving red indentations. He pulled the belt from under me and laid it across the back of my thighs, stretched it tight so that I was pinned. There was a long, voluptuous moment as he regarded my ass, trapped and exposed. And I knew. I realized that he would hold me how I needed to be held; so tight I couldn't escape even if I wanted to. That's when the thought bloomed dark and beautiful—*I've found the one. A man tender enough for pain.*

Today, as he pulls the belt smoothly through the loops in his trousers, it's like our history is strung out along it, in every notch. The dark leather menace of it, the long tail that curls out and stretches in his hands. The forked tongue that promises to sting me.

I waited for months for that promise to become a reality. Back in the early days, he would tell me that I wasn't ready, even when I begged.

"I've played with other men before you, you know."
"And what happened?"
"They...didn't work out."
"Too rough, I bet."
"Rough in the wrong places. They couldn't stick to the rules."
"Well, sugar, I only have one rule."
"Which is?"
"Trust me."

I know what he wants, but I wait for his signal. He never talks. The air is heavy with unspoken words. I used to wish for him to give me instructions, *bitch, say yes, say no, spread your legs for me.* Until I realized that his power lies in his body, not his words. In those strong-boned hands and those quick fingers. His touch is more eloquent than any dirty-mouthed playacting.

His hands are working now. Untying the knot at my waist, pulling roughly at the straps, undoing me. I am in his hands, and love it. He surveys me, roving over the goods, choosing what he wishes to play with first. When he squeezes my breast, he does it hard, pinching my nipple so it flowers in a burst of pain. I allow myself a sharp intake of breath, but any more—a theatrical moan, a plea—and he will let go. So I bite my lip as he rolls the stinging tip of my breast in his fingers, teasing it to stiffness. He touches me with complete intent, knowing what he wants and taking it.

Our silence is complicit. We don't admit that we are playing the game. We never mention it. Since that one summer night, when he asked his final question and I gave my answer, there has been no need.

As he digs his hand under my hip and rolls me onto my front, I become his pet. Like a lapdog, cowering under threat of punishment. I would curl, I would turn in on myself and have him kiss me open again, but that is not his plan.

I know what he wants, and I comply. Jut the buttocks, arch the spine. Lock my limbs in position so I am frozen in the pose. Trapped under him, just as he'd promised I would be. Just as he warned me.

"Remember, there's no going back."
"But what if something goes wrong?"
"Like I said. Trust me."
"This isn't how it's supposed to work."
"Our game, Yvonne. Our rules."
"Your rules."
"Exactly."

I can't see him draw back behind me, nor hear him lick his lips. This is trust, this moment of blind anticipation. Still, he doesn't speak, but when he brings his hand down across my arse and smacks me hard, my skin cries out. Sharp cracks, a rain of blows, a battering of the soft fat curve of my bottom.

A swarming. The rush of wonderful pain that burns over me, warms the open shell of my sex that faces him. The dark wound, the soft spot. The opening where he sinks his fingers, reaches inside me to reiterate—invades me, overtakes me, plunges into me farther than I can reach with his long, searching fingers and their thick knuckles.

A knee shoved between my thighs forces me wider open,

knocks my legs apart like a dance teacher manipulating his pupil. Plié. Facedown.

Now the cock, the battering ram of hard flesh that shunts its way inside me, way deep. I am pinioned, impaled; his cock fills my ass, hips, cunt, belly and reaches for my heart. It flutters in me, sinks and swings. His hips are a wall slamming against me; his balls a weapon, a heavy sac that hits my humming lips a moment after he penetrates me.

His hands? They are how he is working me, clawing at my hips and twisting, mauling the flesh. Working and rubbing at my ass, like he's kneading dough. With every thrust he shoves my face into the sheets, chafing my hanging breasts against the fabric. I can barely breathe, I am being fucked so thoroughly.

Like this, on all fours, I'm tossed around like a cork on stormy waters. He drives me into the mattress, holding on to my hips and drilling, pounding, rutting.

The sharp, clear longing of the time we're aiming for orgasm reminds me of how close we were, when he finally decided the time was right. After three months of exploration, I had to choose. Submit to him, completely, or say good-bye.

"It's nearly time to make up your mind."
"Yes or no?"
"Yes or no."

When his cock turns so rigid it almost hurts, I know he's coming. He releases my hand, and I know what my orders are. My fingers fly to my electric clit, start strumming. This is the crescendo now, the stretch where neither of us is fully human, and the fury of our blood eclipses all thought. The body disappears and becomes only motion, only friction. He gasps, and his voice when I hear it at last is deeper and rawer than ever. A stranger's sounds fly from his throat, animal sounds.

He applies pressure to the base of my spine, angling my hips up so that he can bang as deep as his cock will reach. Under his hand, I twist upward; I open myself to his furious throttle. And as my hand clangs against my clit, percussion, cymbals, and bass drum in my ass with the high sharp keening of the song that he is wringing from my throat. I sing, I cry, I weep.

In that shattered moment, I ache with love. I finally give in, with the same word I used to seal our pact. It's the opposite of a safeword, the only word I could ever say to him, the word that blossoms in my mouth:

"Yes,

yes,

yes..."

MAKE ME

Rachel Kramer Bussel

Something about Gabe brings out the brat in me. The little girl who wears pigtails, sticks out her tongue, and throws tantrums. The grown-up woman who's been longing her whole life for someone to put her in her place, firmly, forcefully. What I love best about him is that he sees right through me, and has since we first met. He's never tolerated my teasing or taunting, never wavered in his belief that what I really need is someone to lead so I can follow, even if I pout the whole while. Ultimately, as bratty as I may act, I know deep down that he knows what's best for me, that'll he'll do everything he can to both protect me and push my buttons. I wouldn't have it any other way, and believe me, I tried for a long while with men far more withholding than Gabe.

I've been a kinky girl ever since I first started getting laid. Fortunately, my first lover was fifteen years older and knew just what to do with his belt—lash it against my tender, nineteen-year-old ass. He made me scream, Bob did, but oh how those

screams have echoed in my head for the last decade, even as
I've learned to scream harder, higher, happier, in my own way.
I love screaming and crying when I bottom, but I've found that
a lot of so-called tops can't quite go there with me; their inner
anxiety about whether I'm really enjoying myself takes over. I
can sympathize, up to a point; I've spanked a few asses along
the way but anything more just doesn't feel right to me. So until
I met Gabe I was looking for someone who'd be my equal, my
complement in kink, and I just so happened to find him.

We met when I was looking for a personal trainer. I'd been
going to big, fancy gyms for years, and I knew all the games I
could play. I realized early on that most of the trainers had good
intentions, but their financial motivation allowed them to let
me get away with slacking off. They were fearful that if they
pushed me too far, I'd stalk off, never to be heard from again,
not quite realizing that what I really needed was to be ordered
around, in a voice that meant business. With them, I could always flutter my naturally long brown lashes and give a sexy
smile to get out of doing the really onerous exercises, the ones
that made me grunt, the ones that I knew were good for me but,
like wheat germ, I just couldn't really stomach. I got by like that
for a long time, never truly pushing myself. I looked good, but
not as good as I could look, and after I'd escaped from the gym,
the high from getting away with doing very little soon wore off.
I wanted someone to *really* kick my ass. Just the thought had
my blood racing, as I walked even faster across the Brooklyn
Bridge, imagining a man literally cracking a whip behind me.
I knew this would never really happen, but a kinky girl can
dream, can't she?

But when my latest trainer moved out to California, I started
searching for a new one. I found Gabe online and, I have to
admit, I was attracted to his body first, before I even read his

credentials and philosophy. Those were in keeping with my ideas about fitness, too; he didn't seem interested in simply pumping out overly muscled men and women, but cared about nutrition and lifelong health as well. I debated what to wear that first day, and settled on a new matching light purple tank top and pants, ones I thought looked good against my skin. I knew that wasn't really the point, but I wanted to look good. Something told me that Gabe was going to become more than my trainer—at least, if I could help it.

He scoffed at me when he saw my attire, insisting that next time I find something else to wear. "Pastels are for pussies," he said, and just hearing him say that second *p*-word had my own aching. "Remember that, doll," he said, making the last word sound like an insult of the highest order. Then he put me to work, with barely any chitchat. I wanted to let my mind wander, meandering from his firm chest down to what he was hiding in his pants, but there was no time to do anything but focus. Right away, we were pumping iron, and he didn't give me an inch. When I started to whine or complain, he got right up in my face. "You're paying me good money to tell *me* how to run things? I don't think so, princess." Every time he got close to me, my heart beat faster, and I pictured him slamming me against the wall, rigging my hands above my head, showing me how he was going to keep me in line—with his cock. I kept picturing him naked, and lucky for me, that helped me lift even more weight.

We continued like that in the following weeks, the tension between us mounting, but neither of us acting on it. I got firmer, stronger, tougher, but inside, I was still looking for the man who could break me, who could make me whimper and sob and submit to him completely. The man who'd make me go to my lowest point, grind me to a pulp, then put me back together again, better than I was before. The man who knew what a girl

like me needed. I hoped Gabe was that man, but part of the
thrill, as maddening as it could be, was waiting for him to make
the first move.

It happened two months later. We were alone late at night
at the gym. Nobody ever came in after nine. The window was
open but nobody was looking at us. We were alone, and even
in the huge gym, that same tension swept over me with every
move. I was doing pull-ups, and after eight weeks of practicing
with a large red rubber strap around my leg as an aid, this time,
it was all about me. Gabe wanted me to learn to do it without
assistance. Ten reps. It doesn't sound like that many, until you
try pulling against a metal bar with all your might and barely
being able to move. I was smaller than I'd been when I joined
his gym, but more muscular, and pulling my own weight up
over the bar was hard. I was about to conk out after three attempts. My arms just hung there stubbornly, and when I tried
to lift myself, my body seemed to get heavier, gravity fiercer.
"Grrr," I said through gritted teeth, like he'd taught me, but
still, I couldn't pull myself up. I'd inch upward a tiny bit, then
drop down, my arms almost useless.

"You can do it," he said, his voice low and encouraging,
good cop for once. I pulled, feeling the strain all through my
arms, gritting my teeth, but just couldn't make it to the top.
My eyes skimmed over the bar, but my chin couldn't get past
it. I dropped down to the wooden box below me and gave him
my patented fluttering eyes/sexy pout combo. He responded by
reaching out and pinching my lower lip, the one I'd thrust out
just that little bit more. His fingers were firm and hard, and
I gasped, but I couldn't deny that my pussy responded just as
firmly as if he'd been touching me there. I'd been pinched before,
but never there, and I'd had no idea that my lips were that sensitive. He kept his hand there, finally dropping it, only to rake

his fingernails down my chin and over my sweaty chest. They were clipped and neat and didn't hurt, but I felt their scrape nonetheless.

"You know what, Jen? You know what you need? I think you are just so used to being a spoiled, selfish, entitled brat who's got every guy she meets wrapped around her little finger that you don't know what to do when someone really pushes you." He'd raised his voice, the vibrations as powerful as his tone. He stepped closer so we were only about three inches apart. His fingers tugged my sports bra and thin white T-shirt downward, causing pressure at the back of my neck. "What if I made you do this workout naked, huh? What if I made you come in here every day and strip in the bathroom and walk out totally bare?" His words hung in the air, totally surreal but nonetheless making me completely, utterly horny. As if by instinct, I glanced to my right, looking out the window and down on Third Avenue. Both of us knew that if I were naked, anyone looking up would see me. He dropped his hand.

"Actually, it's not a question. It's an order. Take off those sweaty clothes. Maybe it'll make it easier to lift yourself up." His eyes surveyed every inch of my body, catching my hard nipples beneath the layers, the outline of my pussy under my tight black workout pants. I wondered if he could tell how completely wet I was.

I wanted to plead for him to change his mind. And, of course, I could've stalked off and walked out, and I didn't think he'd have stopped me. But even more than I wanted to leave, I wanted to stay. I wanted to make him proud—and horny. But I didn't want to give in too easily; I got the feeling he liked that I wasn't a pushover. Instead of begging, I turned defiant. "Make me," I said, the brat in me coming out full force.

"*Make you?* Make you? You know, Jen, I've suspected just

what kind of dirty girl you were since you first walked in here, but now I know for sure. You can damn well bet I'm gonna make you." And with that, he lifted me down from the box, then stripped off my workout pants and my soaked panties in one move. I had to jump out of the way lest he make me trip. "That's better already," he said as he looked down at my bare legs and the dark fuzz covering my pussy. If I'd known I was about to be naked in front of him, I'd have gotten waxed. Then his hand went up my shirt and pinched one nipple through the fabric of the bra. I gasped, but it was clearly a gasp of pleasure. He kept going, his fingers working me just like they'd held my lip, strong and steady. We were so close his leg was touching mine. "You can stop me at any time," he grunted into my ear as he twisted my nipple. "Say 'fire' and I'll stop touching you. But until I hear that, I'm not gonna stop."

He looked deep into my eyes and that's exactly what I saw there—fire. Heat. Lust. He wanted me, but he wanted to make me bend first. He just kept pinching me all over—my nipple, my lip, the inside of my arm. Then lower. My stomach, that thin layer of flesh I'd been trying to shed. Then my hip, and then my clit. It was slippery but he managed to grasp on to it. I gasped but didn't say a word, the warmth spreading throughout my body. I wanted him to fuck me, but I wasn't gonna beg.

"Are you ready yet, Jen? Has this been motivation enough? Because I'm gonna make you do it before you leave here tonight, no matter what. And if you wait until after I fuck you, it's just gonna be all the more difficult. You might want to conserve your strength." While he was speaking, his fingers had moved from my clit down to my wetness, tracing it, navigating along my lips, testing me further. I wanted to give in, but I couldn't just yet.

Then he lifted me up and put me back on the box. "Put

your hands on the bar and hang there. I'll be right back," he
said, and, like a robot, I did it. Unlike a robot, I was soaking wet, my heart pounding, my mouth dry yet hungry. I was
torn between my natural brattiness and the spell he'd cast on
me. When he returned, he had an evil grin on his face, and a
purple butt plug and bottle of lube in his hands. "I think I was
too easy on you before. Now I want you to do it with this up
your ass. That'll make it more interesting, don't you think?" I
nodded, and let him wrap his arms around my waist and lead
me to the ground.

"Get on your hands and knees. Like a dog," he said, add-
ing the last bit because by then he could see how every time
he slighted me, I got off on it. He didn't tell me to spread my
legs, he just pressed them apart until my ass was way up in the
air, my legs spread wide, the breeze greeting my pussy. Then
he poured the lube directly between my cheeks. I felt the cool
liquid sink between them, working its way into my puckered
hole. "That's it, Jen," he said in the voice he uses to encourage
me when he knows I'm almost there with my exercises. "I have
a feeling you'll like this." Then he was pushing the head of the
plug inside me. I let my head drop and my ass rise to meet the
toy, and while I wiggled, he pressed, until it was snugly between
my cheeks. Then he gave them each one firm, strong slap.

"Yeah," I whispered into the air.

"No more spanking until you do what I want you to," he
said. "You're paying me, remember?" When I realized that it
was true, I was indeed paying him—not to fuck me, exactly, but
we were still technically on the clock—a fresh wave of humiliation, oh-so-arousing humiliation, swept over me. It was one
thing to want a man to dominate me, but to pay him for the
privilege? I was truly perverted, and the thought made me practically come on the spot.

And that's the thing. In the end, he made me, but really, I made myself. I hoisted my horny, sweaty, naked body up over that pole, again and again, energized not by rage or humiliation but pure lust. The butt plug only egged me on, not moving, just sitting there, reminding me that my ass was his in every way. My ass, my arms, my back, my legs, and most of all, my mind, my soul, were his for the taking. Because he'd earned it. Because he'd made me want to fight, want to snarl, want to be the bratty girl who gets what's coming to her. And as I raised and lowered myself, I felt a different kind of fire burning through me, one that somehow connected my arms and back to my pussy, giving me strength I didn't even know I had. By then, I almost wanted someone to be watching, wanted someone to see just what I could do, what Gabe could get me to do. What we were about to do together. By then I was in my own zone, and went far beyond the ten reps he'd initially demanded. When I finally stepped back down, my body shaking from exertion, I felt like I was in a trance.

I was no longer his brat or his sub or his underling; I was an equal partner in this tug-of-war we were just about to start. I was naked and he was clothed, but suddenly, that didn't matter. "You're something else, you know that, Jen?" he said, chuckling as I stood there, waiting for him to direct me. "I think we're going to make that butt plug a permanent part of our workouts. But I don't want to train you here anymore. It's just not right. We're moving our sessions to the bedroom. At least, after tonight, we are. Right now I think you need to get back on your knees." I did, immediately, jumping down off the box and returning to my kneeling position. He gave me his cock to taste, and I slowly licked around the tip, but only for a moment, before he joined me on the floor. He guided his fingers between my legs, finding me totally wet. I leaned my head against his shoulder, most of my energy gone but my arousal through the roof, the plug still in place, growing increasingly insistent that I respond to its touch. My pussy clenched, quickly followed by my back door, as Gabe sank his fingers deep inside me.

"Come, Jen, come on my hand, give it to me," he said.

"Make me," I said, stifling a giggle as his strokes increased in urgency. "Make me." And just like the first time I'd uttered those two words, that's exactly what he did.

BODY ELECTRIC

Lisabet Sarai

For GCS, on his birthday

He didn't look like an engineer. He smiled and postured and gestured expansively, as if reciting poetry or making a speech. Half a dozen females surrounded him, hanging on his every word. Periodically, the little knot of women (which actually included crusty old Margaret Evans) would burst into self-conscious laughter. Dean Evans would look around nervously, then return her attentive gaze to the towering shaggy-haired orator in their midst, as if he were a combination of Tom Cruise and Mahatma Gandhi.

A politician, or a TV celebrity, or even the leader of a cult: I could readily believe that he was any of these as I watched him fascinate his listeners. But an assistant professor from the department of electrical engineering? Highly implausible, but true nevertheless. Earlier in the evening, my colleague Loren had given me a full briefing. Dr. Ryan Moresby was apparently a brilliant teacher and talented inventor, and a rising star in his department. In addition, Loren emphasized, he was single, which was surprising considering his obvious talent in attracting the opposite sex. Of course, why would someone with that kind of charisma want to settle down?

I wondered idly how many of the women in that little circle of his he had bedded, then gave myself a mental slap on the hand. I had to stop thinking like that! Ever since I completed my dissertation, I had found myself speculating on other people's secret lives and desires. My research on women's erotic literature was, of course, impeccably scholarly, serious and restrained, carefully purged of any salacious elements. My sources, though, were anything but. Their enduring influence on my thoughts was only too clear.

Richard had been so embarrassed by my research he could hardly bear to mention it. I used to tease him when we were in bed together, threatening to tell him some of the stories I had been reading and writing about during the day. He'd stop my voice with a desperate kiss. For Richard, a scholar in the field of medieval history, sex was something you did, not something you talked about. It was a function of the body, enjoyable, fulfilling, necessary, but ultimately subordinate to the life of the mind.

These days, though, my mind was continually being hauled back to the topic of sex. Being apart from Richard was a major factor, of course. It's a long way from Gainesville to Manitoba. He phoned me at least once a week, but that was hardly satisfying. Richard would find the notion of phone sex appalling. I loved Richard, and had missed him terribly during these first months at my new job, but I had to admit he was annoyingly prudish.

At this point, I sometimes wished I'd chosen another thesis topic. I was teaching Feminist Thought and Culture as well as the freshman composition course, but I knew the nickname the students had bestowed on me.

"You! Come over here." I started, my meditations interrupted by a rich, unfamiliar voice. The female crowd around Moresby had dispersed, and sure enough, he was beckoning to me.

Rude, I thought, but I obeyed him anyway.

"I don't know you, do I?" He smiled down at me. My brief irritation at his lack of manners melted away in the heat of that smile.

"I'm Colette D'Arpignay. I just joined the Department of Languages and Literature this semester."

"Oh, right! The Sex Professor!"

I felt the blood rising in my cheeks. "Oh dear! I didn't realize that had spread outside my own department."

"Never mind. It doesn't hurt to have a bit of a racy reputation. Makes you more interesting." He scanned my body, not even trying to disguise his lascivious interest. "The question is, do you deserve it?"

My earlobes burned. Despite the air conditioning, sweat trickled down between my breasts. I was acutely aware of my tightened nipples pressing against the purple jersey of my top. I couldn't look at him.

He leaned over like a conspirator and delicately flicked one terribly obvious bud with his forefinger. A bolt of lightning sizzled through me and ignited a sudden blaze between my thighs.

"I'm willing to bet that you do deserve it," he murmured, close to my ear.

I pulled back, stumbling on my high heels, trying to regain control. "Please, Dr. Moresby. Remember where we are." He did not look in the least repentant. "I'd rather not talk about it."

"Oh?" He looked at me skeptically, eyebrows raised. "I'm

not sure I believe that. Anyway, call me Ryan." He dug in his pocket and produced a slightly crumpled business card. "Here's my card."

I took it, reluctantly, somehow unable to refuse it.

"And may I have yours, Colette?" His eyes seized mine and wouldn't let me look away. Later I couldn't remember their color—only their intensity.

It seemed that I was moving in dreamlike slow motion as I extracted a card from my purse and handed it to him. He nodded. "Good. It's got both your office and your cell. We'll talk soon."

Dean Evans appeared, with a busty, fortysomething blonde in tow. "Excuse me for interrupting, Ryan, but I must introduce you to Larissa Carter, from Biology. She just came to us from UC San Francisco."

"Dr. Carter." He took her hand and half-bowed. "I'm delighted to meet you." She looked as charmed as everyone else by him. I wondered if he'd tweak her nipples, too.

I turned to go, but his hand on my arm stopped me. I was wearing long sleeves, but somehow I felt as though he was touching my bare skin. "Don't forget, Colette. I want to hear all about your research."

"And I want to learn about yours," I replied archly.

"Oh, you will," he said with a strange smile, and then turned the magic of his attention back to the buxom biologist.

My legs were a bit shaky. I got myself another glass of wine and found a seat near the windows. In a moment, Loren joined me, waving a pink silk fan back and forth in front of her face.

"Whew, it's hot. They should turn up the AC." She sipped at her wine. "Anyway, what did he say? What did you think of him?"

"What did I think of whom?"

"Moresby, of course. I saw you talking to him."

"He somehow manages to be charming even when he's arrogant and rude."

"Really? Well, I guess when you're that brilliant you have the right to be arrogant."

"Maybe. I wouldn't know."

Loren gave a throaty laugh. "Oh, Colette, drop the false modesty. How many other junior professors already have a book on their CV? And a best seller at that!"

Richard had been mortified when he heard about my publication deal. "Please, Loren..."

"So? Tell all!"

"We hardly exchanged two sentences." I blushed, recollecting his piercing gaze and bold touch.

"Well, I think he's sexy."

"Sexy? Maybe. I didn't really notice."

I could put Loren off, but I couldn't lie to myself. During the next few days, the dark, audacious engineer appeared often in my thoughts and fantasies. I remembered his physical presence, the aura of attraction that surrounded him. I mentally replayed our conversation, devising all sorts of witty or withering ripostes to his challenges.

Whenever the phone rang, I both hoped and worried that it might be him. The engineering building was on the other end of campus from my office, but each time I saw a tall male figure striding across one of the quads, my stomach tied itself in a knot and my nipples began to ache.

As the days went by without any contact, though, I began to relax. He must have just been teasing me. He must come on to all women like that. Flirtation. Temptation. I'm sure we all respond to that kind of innuendo, the implication that we're special, the suggestion that we have secret desires that he alone understands and can fulfill.

Late Friday afternoon I was in my office expecting a call from Richard and I picked the phone up on the first ring.

"You're certainly eager, Colette." At the sound of his voice, my whole body blushed.

"Um, Dr. Moresby. Ryan. I didn't think you were going to call."

"Oh? I told you that we'd talk. I always keep my word."

"Oh, well..."

"Were you sorry not to hear from me? Did you miss me?"

I was silent. How could I possibly answer?

"Don't pretend. I know you've been thinking of me." What an arrogant bastard! But of course, it was true. "I've been thinking about you, too, ever since that party. Thinking about what I'd like to do to you."

"Do? To me?" I barely managed to squeak out the words.

"Oh yes. I have ideas. Lots of ideas. First of all, I'd like to remove your clothes. Very slowly, one piece at a time."

I choked on sudden panic. I should hang up.

"You'll just stand there and allow me to undress you. You're not allowed to stop me."

Not allowed? I was on the phone with a virtual stranger, who was making obscene comments. I should hang up immediately, and then maybe even call the police. I couldn't, though. All I could do was clutch the handset and listen, fascinated and horrified.

"When you're completely naked, I think that I'll tie you up. You'd like that, wouldn't you?"

"What? No. Of course not."

"Don't lie to me, Colette. I've read your book."

"My book is a scholarly exploration of women's sexual attitudes as revealed in their fiction..."

"Bull turds. Your book is a mirror of who you truly are."

"No, I..."

"You must be honest with me. You must always tell me the truth. You can trust me, Colette. I won't judge you. I see who you are. I celebrate who you are."

There was a gentleness in his voice now. I felt myself melting, despite the awful tension.

"I'll bind you to the table with nice, smooth, cotton cords. I have a special table that I've designed, just for this. Just for you. It's upholstered in soft, padded leather, and has lots of attachment points. For ropes and other sorts of bonds. You'll like it."

I tried for sarcasm and failed dismally. "Of course I'll like it, being trussed up like a turkey ready for stuffing."

My voice trembled and broke. The fact was, I could see the scene he was describing; see my pale, bare skin, ropes around my wrists and ankles, my arms and legs spread wide, my pussy gaping and exposed.

I gripped the phone so hard that my joints hurt. My palms were clammy. My breathing was ragged. And I was painfully, shamefully aware of how swollen and damp my pussy had become in response to this frightening and exciting mental picture.

"Ready for stuffing!" His laugh was musical and mocking. "Oh yes, that's good. I'd love to stuff you, Colette. Just think about all the things I might stuff you with. Carrots. Cucumbers. A broomstick. A baseball bat." Everything he said, I saw. I shuddered, but my cunt betrayed me, contracting eagerly at the notion of these violations.

"My cock, of course, I'll reserve for last. First, I need to introduce you to my apparatus."

"Your—apparatus?"

"I have a variety of inventions that I'm sure you'll find entertaining."

He sounded like a mad scientist.

"As I said, I'm eager to share my research with you." He stopped and listened for a moment, as if trying to gauge my reactions. "Colette, are you still there?"

"Uh—yes, I'm here."

"Good. So when can we start?"

"Start?"

"You don't have to come to my place the first time. It might make you a bit...nervous. Why don't I drop by your apartment tonight?"

"Tonight? But I can't. I have to work. And, anyway I have a boyfriend."

"But do you have a lover?"

The way he said the word sent a cold thrill through my body.

"I know you won't disappoint me, Colette. I'll see you at eight. Be ready for me."

As soon as he hung up I disconnected the phone. It took fifteen minutes for my breathing to return to normal. I had to leave by the back door so that nobody would see the wet patch on the back of my skirt.

Be ready, he had said. I sat on my couch, wondering what that meant. Should I shower and shave my legs? Should I put on the corset and thong I bought for that Halloween party? The one Richard wouldn't let me wear? Should I take my clothes off completely?

I was not completely naive. I knew the BDSM clichés from working on my thesis. I had read many stories where women were bound, beaten, even branded. Stories where pain led to transcendent pleasure. This was nothing like those stories.

Ready. I shut my eyes and tried to slow my racing heartbeat, breathing deeply as if I were in yoga class. My mind betrayed me, projecting vivid images on my closed eyelids. Images of naked flesh marked with the scarlet tracks of a whip. Images of obscenely stretched limbs and orifices distended by foreign objects. Ryan had mentioned his "apparatus." I imagined a towering framework of steel and leather, hung with cables and chains, designed to constrain a body in a hundred impossible, degrading positions. New moisture seeped out of my sex, staining the sofa.

Ultimately, I just sat, waiting. After a while, the dreadful excitement subsided to a slight breathlessness, an inner trembling, a fluttering between my thighs. I wanted to touch myself, to relieve some of the tension, but I knew from my reading that I shouldn't. I was no longer allowed to satisfy myself.

He didn't knock or ring the bell. He simply entered my apartment through the unlocked door, as if it was his right to be there. His nostrils flared as he came into the living room. He sniffed appreciatively and smiled at me, looking amused. That smile made me want to sink to my knees in front of him. Maybe that was what I should do? But somehow I couldn't move. He stood by the couch, towering over me. I watched him, searching for cues.

"Colette." He held out his hand, big enough to swallow mine completely. He raised me to my feet, still holding me with his eyes. I thought for a moment that he would kiss me, but the moment passed. Disappointment flooded me. How could I please him?

"Should I—do I have to call you Master?" He grinned at me. I thought I'd die of embarrassment.

"Do you want to?"

"Um...I don't think so. It would seem artificial."

"Well, then. It's your choice, you know. This is all your choice."

I couldn't believe that. I felt compelled by him, controlled by his will, ensnared by his lecherous mind.

"Why don't you just address me as 'Sir'? Or better yet, how about 'Doctor'?" His smile was half-mocking, half-gentle. "How would that be?"

"That would be fine—Doctor."

"Excellent. But you shouldn't say anything unless I give you permission. You know that, don't you?"

I nodded. This seemed like the natural order of things.

"Good. Now, then. Let's get rid of those clothes."

I began to unbutton my blouse. "No, don't move. I'll undress you, this time."

He undid the first three buttons and pulled the garment open to reveal my unglamorous cotton bra. He brushed his fingertips over my swollen nipples, clearly visible as they poked against the fabric. Pleasure shivered across my skin and down to my already aching pussy.

"You have such lovely big nipples. So sensitive." He pinched the right one. I gasped. "I don't want you to wear a bra anymore. I want everyone to be able to see those luscious tits of yours."

"But, when I teach...it's not proper..."

"Did I say you could speak?" He frowned briefly. I wanted to drop through the floor.

"If you want to please me, you'll go braless. It's up to you."

I was silent. I craved his approval, more than anything.

He laid a cool palm against my cheek. "What other people think doesn't matter, Colette. You only need to worry about me."

All at once he leaned down and kissed me. I expected brashness, energy, power. Instead it was a gossamer kiss, delicate, the barest contact of his lips on mine.

It set me on fire. Tremors raced through my body. I felt his hands everywhere, exploring, exposing my raw need. I felt his mind, questing, tasting the flavors of my lust. Yet only his lips were touching me, and just barely.

I wanted more. I wanted his tongue, his fingers. I wanted his cock, which I knew was hard though I hadn't seen it. I was acutely aware of his lust, controlled and hidden as it was. I tried to press my body against him, but he pulled away.

"Not yet. Not until you're ready." He resumed the process of methodically removing my clothes. He did not touch me again. I could swear that he was trying to frustrate me. I promised myself that I wouldn't beg.

Finally, I was naked. He stepped back to look me over. "Very nice. Even nicer than I imagined. You have such fair skin, Colette. The blood is very close to the surface."

Blood? I remembered that I hardly knew this man. Somehow that was irrelevant.

"And you're so hairy, down here. I'm glad you're not shaved. Although that might heighten the sensations, I admit that I'm somewhat old-fashioned." He slipped a finger through the curly tangle of my pubic hair, unerringly finding my clit. Sparks shot through me. My body jerked uncontrollably.

He took his hand away. I prayed silently that he'd put it back.

"So very wet, too. That's excellent. It will raise the conductivity."

Conductivity?

"The bedroom is this way, correct?"

I nodded, not wanting to speak unless absolutely necessary. He picked up an attaché case and gestured toward my room. "Well then, let's try in there. I don't see any appropriate attachment points in here."

My room was dim, lit only by the lamp on my bureau. I
stood awkwardly in the middle of the floor, at a loss, while Ryan
reconnoitered. My clit was still tingling from his brief exploration. My juices dribbled lazily down the insides of my thighs.

"I think I see how to manage this. Lie down here."

He rummaged in his case while I arranged myself on the
bed. He held up a thick coil of cotton clothesline. A stab of fear
distracted me from my arousal. Fantasizing about bondage was
fine, but could I really allow him to do this?

"I am going to tie you to the bed, Colette, unless you tell me
to stop. You don't have to be afraid. I've done this many times
before."

Jealousy flared up, replacing the fear. Who else had he used
the way he was using me?

"So, I'm just another conquest for you?" Ryan looked surprised at my outburst. He sat down beside me on the bed and
took my hand.

"No, of course not. You know better than that. You know
that you're special."

"I'm sure that you tell every one of your women that."

"But it's true. I knew it the moment I saw you. You have
a precious gift, a sexual intensity that you can't hide, though
you try. A craving for the extremes of sensation. Overwhelming
curiosity and insatiable appetite. The rare ability to surrender
completely to pleasure."

His touch was making me weak, but I still tried to resist.

"In the stories, the doms always say that. They know how to
push the right buttons. They seduce their victims into thinking
that there's something magical and deep about their interaction.
When after all, it's just sex—kinky, perverted, but in the final
analysis, just sex."

"Just sex?" Ryan leaped onto the bed, straddling my body,

pinning my wrists to the sheets with his huge hands. Then he kissed me with a ferocity that literally took my breath away. His tongue forced its way into my mouth and tangled with mine. He gnawed at my lips, mashing them against my teeth. I tasted blood.

I struggled against him for a moment, then relaxed and let his mouth ravage me. With that release came pleasure so acute that it washed away all thought. I was floating in a sea of pleasure: the tingling in my nipples where his shirt rubbed against them, the sparks flashing across my belly from the pressure of his hidden cock, the exquisite contractions rippling through the depths of my cunt.

I writhed against him, unable to control myself, not caring what he thought or what he did. I opened myself to the pleasure and let it take me away.

"'And if the body does not do as much as the Soul? And if the body were not the Soul, what is the Soul?'"

Ryan had relinquished my mouth and was peering down at me. His long black hair half-obscured his blazing eyes.

I gasped for breath. "Walt Whitman. *Leaves of Grass*." The pleasure had subsided somewhat, but I knew that it lay waiting for me to claim it again.

"Yes. 'Books, art, religion, time, the visible and solid earth, the atmosphere and the clouds, and what was expected of heaven or fear'd of hell, are now consumed.' That's what he was talking about, you know. Sex. 'Just' sex."

I nodded. I knew.

"Let me bind you, Colette."

I nodded again.

My bed had no hooks, no attachment points. Ryan simply fastened one end of the rope around my wrist, then threaded it under the bed and up the other side to wrap my other wrist. He

secured my ankles in a similar manner. Simple and efficient. I
lay quietly, feeling the pleasure trembling beneath the surface
whenever he touched me.

Before long he stood over me. I assumed that he was admiring his handiwork.

I had imagined this, but the reality was far more intense.
I was helpless, unable to move or escape. Truly in his power.
My body was displayed, shameless, available for him to use in
any way he desired. I had never been more frightened. Or more
excited.

"Comfortable? Are the ropes too tight?"

I shook my head. My legs were spread wide, my cunt lips
stretched open, baring my throbbing clit to tremble in random
air currents. The sheet beneath me was soaked with my secre-
tions. *Do something,* I thought. *Anything.*

He returned to his attaché case. There was a strange noise,
a kind of hissing or snapping. "I thought we might begin with
this little gadget."

The thing in his hands looked like something from a 1940s
horror film. It had a handle, topped with a mushroom-shaped
globe of glass that glowed with a malevolent purple light. Inside
the glass, bright sparks danced. Their images flickered on the
wall next to the bed.

Slowly, he brought the bulb closer to my bare flesh. The
crackling noise grew more intense. He hovered above my nipple.
"Don't move," he whispered.

All at once a rain of sparks shot from the tube to the taut
node of flesh. I was being pierced with a thousand needles. I
screamed, as much from surprise as from the pain. Ryan pulled
the device away, as I tried to catch my breath.

"Colette?"

"Sorry, Doctor. I wasn't expecting..." Before I could finish, his mouth was on my recently assaulted nipple, lapping and sucking, soaking my skin with his hot saliva. I felt every movement of his tongue deep in my cunt. When he brought the glowing globe close again, I thought I was ready. This time, though, the sparks were stronger, hotter, more painful. Electricity crawled over my breast, wherever he had left traces of wetness.

Before I could recover, he was sparking my other nipple. I jumped and squirmed. My cunt contracted with each contact. He stroked my stomach. "You're all sweaty," he said. The thing sputtered and popped. Miniature bolts of lightning showered down on my navel. "And your thighs are smeared with cunt juice..." He swept the wand slowly over my body and a long trail of sparks stitched up the sensitive skin toward my gaping sex.

"I've always been fascinated by electricity," he said in a conversational tone as the bulb approached my cunt. I tensed, waiting for the jolt I knew would come. Nothing could have prepared me for the raw sensations. Sparks danced on my clit and sputtered among my wet folds. I screamed again, overwhelmed, confused as to whether I was in terrible pain or close to climax.

My tormenter paused. "I didn't invent this handy little device, but I've made a few modifications. For example, I can turn up the power, or increase the frequency. Or make the variations random. Would you like that?"

All I could do was moan.

"But this is my favorite innovation." He held up a pair of gloves, made from some translucent material. "Carbon nanotube fiber. Got it from a friend in the materials engineering department. Flexible, essentially indestructible, and highly conductive. So I can switch to one of the cylinder-shaped tubes, like this, and then hold on with one hand, like this, and then my every touch becomes electric."

He touched one gloved finger to my aching clit. Current surged through me, different than before, sharper and deeper. "I can shock your nipples, or your earlobes." He demonstrated, each charge stronger and more intense than the previous one. "I've programmed the power unit for an increasing ramp," he said with a smile.

He trailed his free hand down between my breasts to my belly. A cascade of sparks followed the path of his fingers. I twitched and writhed, tears welling in my eyes. "I could do the same thing with bare hands, but the carbon-based gloves make the sensations stronger and more focused."

"What I really like, though, is to do this." He plunged three fingers deep into my cunt. The power unit hissed. Electricity sizzled through my moist flesh, waking every nerve, burning away the last shreds of control. My muscles clamped down on his hand. My clit pulsed wildly. He hit me with another jolt. Energy arced through me. I thrashed and struggled against my bonds, jerking like a rag doll as I came again and again and yet again.

Ryan was unfastening the ropes when I struggled back to some semblance of consciousness. My wrists hurt. "You chafed them a bit," he said apologetically. "I didn't realize how strongly you'd react. We'll have to get you some nice lined cuffs, so you don't do more damage."

My whole body felt limp, light, transparent. My mind was strangely blank. Doctor Moresby climbed onto the bed and cradled me in his lap, stroking my hair.

"Are you okay, Colette? You may speak now." But I just nodded.

"Did you enjoy it?" I smiled shyly and dropped my eyes. Enjoy was such weak word. He raised my face to his and kissed me gently.

The telephone began to ring.

"That will be Richard." I was surprised to discover that I could talk after all.

"Do you want to answer it?" He seemed to know who I meant.

"What would I say? I really don't know." The ringing went on and on. I snuggled against Ryan's chest. I suddenly felt his erection poking up against my ass. "You're still hard. Do you want...? Can I...?"

"Later. There's no rush." Idly, he began to play with my breasts, strumming the nipples with one finger. The sparks had left them unbelievably sensitive. I squirmed in his lap, noticing with a smile how this made him harder.

"Tell me. Tell me about your research. Your apparatus."

"Wouldn't you rather be surprised?"

"I'm sure that hearing about it, and experiencing it, will be quite different."

"Well..." His hand began to travel gradually down the length of my body. "I've adapted the design of a common TENS unit to be a great deal more flexible and adaptable."

"TENS?"

"Transcutaneous Electro-Neural Stimulation. Basically a controllable shock generator. Much more powerful than the Violet Wand."

A delicious shiver traveled up my spine.

"Anyway, I've developed a whole range of specialized attachments. Clamps. Probes. Needles. A pair of stainless steel dildos, so that you can be fucked front and rear while you're being shocked." His fingers were dabbling in my cunt now, his thumb occasionally brushing my clit, bringing memories of shocks, new sparks.

"I'm working on a motorized unit, so that I can synchronize

the thrusts and the charge release. I'm very interested in the effects of anal electrical stimulation." One finger worked its way into my rear hole, raising a whole range of new sensations. I closed my eyes, losing myself again, letting him take me over.

I must have made some small sound of pleasure.

"What are you thinking, Colette?"

My eyes met his, so bright, almost the eyes of a fanatic. Another orgasm shimmered on my body's horizon. I wanted to give up everything for this, for him.

"I'm wondering, how much is sex worth? How much should you be willing to sacrifice, to endure?"

"You mean, for just sex?" With the skill of an expert he pinched my clit and sent me tumbling over the edge and into ecstasy. "I don't know, my love. You tell me."

RECLAIMING THE SOFA

Maddy Stuart

Despite everything, I still flinch at the word *slut*. It's the same with *whore* and *cunt* and the rest of them—despite all the *this-isn't-for-real* assurances in the world, some part of me, the good-girl or the assertive-woman part, wants to flash her eyes and spit a retort. But I think that's what he likes about me.

He's standing over me now, his beautiful body visible only in silhouette. I'm stretched out face-forward on the sofa, which is just short enough to force me to lay my ankles on the armrest. My limbs are an awkward tumble, one arm trailing on the floor and the other dangling over the end of the sofa. My legs are stretched to their greatest length, just the way he asked. He told me over the phone, while struggling to strike the right balance between "friendly conversation" and "phone sex," that he preferred not to tie me up. The sight of me voluntarily arranging my body according to his wishes, he said, was a far greater sign of respect.

We're meeting in my apartment this time, although he won't be seeing what's in my bedroom. I have yet to see what's in his.

My roommate is away for the weekend—a rare occasion—and I'm nearly giddy at the prospect of claiming the living room as mine. It's the last frontier of my apartment, the one room in which I've never been openly, lazily naked; its virginity has been preserved by my roommate's ubiquitous presence on the sofa.

Careful not to alter my pose, I turn my head to the side, just enough to see the length of his cock dipping toward me, lightly brushing my lips. He's leaning over the sofa, propping himself with his arms against the back, and bending his knees just enough to allow me to reach for his cock with my tongue.

"My slut," he calls me, and I part my lips slightly in protest, drawing my breath in quickly. But I remind myself to remain silent, and soon my lips taste of salt as he bends his knees and pushes his cock past my teeth and against my tongue. I yearn to reach out my hand and stroke his lean thighs and his ass that seems the perfect size for my hands, but today is the day for getting what I want, not taking it. He rests his hand lightly on the back of my head, shifting to support himself with the other arm, and fondles my hair with his fingers. He doesn't need to be firm—he knows and I know that he will lead, and I will follow, like ballroom dancers. He grunts and I tilt my head to take him in farther.

It used to be the other way around between us. Our first meeting involved me plundering his ass with a purple dildo strapped to my hips, heaping upon him all the words and phrases I'm now learning not to abhor. I gorged myself on his body, took fistfuls of everything that pleased me, relished his moans and raked my fingernails across his back. He, now, is much gentler and more restrained than I was. Perhaps I should be grateful for this, but sometimes I think that struggles and whimpering entreaties would be a lesser thing to demand from me than the stillness that I am giving him now.

Over the phone one night, when I had just finished listening
to him orgasm after calling him my fuck toy and demanding
that he beg for me to fuck him harder, he suggested that we
try switching places. I was hesitant at first. My last experience
submitting to a man was what I referred to as a "pie-eating
contest"—the man had constantly demanded thicker toys, more
toys; deeper, harder...as if his only goal was to see how much
flesh and silicone could be stuffed inside me at once. It seemed
childish to me, a grotesque spectacle, and I told him I wanted no
such experience again. My current boyfriend assured me that he
would be different.

The first time we met, poor planning had left both of us
sober. We ransacked the cupboards of his friend's apartment
where we'd arranged to have our tryst, looking for something
to wear down the nervous edges. But the little apartment wasn't
mine and wasn't his, neither of us knew where to look, and
we came up empty-handed save for something that claimed to
contain alcohol but had the flavor and potency of grape juice.
So the rough edges stayed, and with each thrust my hands fe-
verishly sought a new patch of skin to maul, a new word to call
him. He simply shuddered and moaned.

This time, the second physical meeting for us, I'm pleasantly
intoxicated. He has the same purple dildo in his hand that I
savaged him with on our first meeting. It curves up and its head
is enlarged, making me think it was designed to penetrate a
woman. If so, now we are returning things to the natural order.
But a few hours before he arrived, for safety's sake, I boiled the
dildo in a pot on the stove, and the sight of the disembodied
purple lump of plastic bobbing up and down in the pot made
me giggle. It seemed wrong to giggle at something that was supposed to tame me.

My legs are splayed haphazardly on the sofa, knees bent, one foot on the floor. He's withdrawn his cock but it still bobs just in front of my face, occasionally brushing against my lips or my cheek. Leaning over, he strokes my pussy with a knob-knuckled finger before easing it inside. I squirm and stretch a little, suddenly thinking of my roommate and relishing my conquest of the living room sofa.

"Stay still, whore," he tells me, and my face turns red while a lightning bolt shoots through my gut at the sound of that word. *I'm not a whore,* I want to tell him, *you know I'm not.* But I know the word is meant to prod, is meant to thrill, is meant to make my insides burn and boil with the contradiction of accepting the poses and the words he is choosing for me tonight. It's been quite some time since I've felt the thrill and the burn so acutely.

His finger is all the way in now and my chest is heaving. He smiles at the sight of all of this—it's not stillness he wants so much as the appearance of restraint, the tension of desire barely controlled, the signs that I'm desperate to get up and either pull his cock inside me or slap him in the face. My foot flinches, my leg straightens and kicks, and his smile turns to a grin. He removes his finger, climbs on the sofa, leans his whole weight against me, and covers my mouth with the newly freed hand. I can feel his cock against my belly and the sofa suddenly seems like my natural domain and his movement a forceful conquest. His finger smells of my juices and I finally give in to the urge to push back against him, squirm and struggle like a damsel in distress, take all the things from him that I took so freely the last time. But he's having none of it. He slaps my breast, hard. I feel the lightning bolts again, and the living room that has never really been mine has become, suddenly and completely, his. So I loosen, stretch my body out, arch my back, and spread my legs as wide as I can.

The dildo that was so recently an amusing lump of plastic boiling in a pot on the stove is now making its way inside my cunt, and I feel my body strain, then relax. His hand over my mouth means that I can moan as much as I like. I hope he can feel my hot breath against it as I try to tell him how much I'm burning up with desire, how the heat coursing through my body seems to follow a trail from my clit to my gut to the base of my throat to the tongue I'm licking his fingers with. It all comes out as grunts and moans, of course, nothing like the soliloquies I was prone to when he was under my hands. But he acts as though his mastery of my body is so complete that the moans are as articulate as the soliloquies, and when he removes his hand from my mouth in order to better position the dildo, I do not speak but simply hum with desire, like a purring cat.

Once the dildo is fully buried, he stands up, moves to the end of the sofa, and draws his cock to my lips. I take the opportunity to look the beautiful angles of his body up and down, the way I did when I was about to make it mine. I remember when the sculpted shoulders were mine to push down, the hips mine to grab hold of, the ankles mine to clutch. I feel a playful insolence creeping into my gaze, one that silently reminds him that if I am a slut, so is he; that we are each other's plaything and that it's only the sofas of friends that have been conquered. In response, he smiles deviously, takes hold of my ankle, and tells me, "Still," before he gives my inner thigh a hard, stinging slap.

But I can abide no more stillness, and instead of clenching my teeth, I let out a loud yelp. He grins, raises his hand again, and lands a second one in the same spot. At that moment I know he's been waiting for me to burst, waiting for me to show him every nuance of the effect he has on me. After a third smack, he pulls the dildo out again, straddles me, pushes my shoulders down, and plunges his own cock, which is so beautiful I could never, never giggle at it, as deep inside me as it will go.

Now, I buck and wriggle and groan to my heart's content while he fucks me with the measured, forceful strength of one who is completely assured of his mastery.

"Are you my slut?" he asks.

"Yes, I'm your slut," I tell him, and find myself relishing the words.

HOW BAD DO YOU WANT IT?

Gwen Masters

I sat in the middle of the rumpled bed. The sounds of silence were all around me—the ticking of the clock, the call of a distant bird, the lack of footsteps in the hallway. Wayne had ordered me to stay naked, said he would be right back, and left me there. That was an hour ago.

My bare breasts felt heavy in my hands. The red marks on them were beginning to fade. Wayne had used the new whip, the one that bit like fire. I had closed my eyes and counted the strokes out loud, waiting for the moment when he would decide I had had enough. My wedding ring was cool against my over-heated skin.

Wayne liked suspense. He loved to hold the whip above my skin, moving it just enough to stir up the tiniest breeze, then bringing it down when I least expected it. He loved to lull me into a feeling of security, then test me by pushing the boundaries. No one would know what I enjoyed just from looking at me. None of my friends knew the way things were. Only I understood that when I disappeared behind closed doors, being submissive wasn't just a desire, it was a need—it was what kept me ready to face the world.

Tired of waiting for him, I lay down and closed my eyes. I dozed on the bed until I awoke to the familiar crunch of tires on the gravel driveway.

Wayne whistled his way into the bedroom. He smiled when he saw I was still naked, just as he had left me. He sat on the bed behind me and snuggled close, pulling me back against his broad chest.

"I went to Blake's house," he said as he kissed my ear.

"How is Blake?" I asked.

Wayne's hand slid down my belly, seeking the place between my legs. I opened my thighs for him. When he spoke, his voice was sensuous and filled with promise.

"Blake is looking forward to seeing you, baby."

I sat very still. The tone of my husband's voice said all I needed to know, but it took a moment for it to sink in. Wayne said nothing else, just rested his lips lightly on my shoulder, waiting for the thoughts to form in my head. He knew I wouldn't say no—if Wayne wanted me to do something, I would do it. It was my pleasure to please him. We had never talked about having another man in bed with us, but Wayne wasn't one to let me know all that was on his mind, either. He liked surprises just as much as he liked suspense.

"I know you like him," Wayne said softly. "I've seen the way you look at him."

"That doesn't mean..."

"I've never questioned your faithfulness."

The silence fell between us. The ticking of the clock was very loud. Wayne simply sat and listened to it while he let me sort through my thoughts. There was an impossible jumble of them.

"Can I ask a question?" I said.

"Go ahead."

"Why?"

Wayne seemed prepared for any question I might ask, save that one. It took him aback.

"Why?" he repeated.

"Yes. Why?"

Wayne contemplated that while his hands slid up and down my arms.

"You know it doesn't make me happy when you question me."

"Yes," I said.

Wayne kissed my shoulder. "I could say it's about pleasing me. I could say it's about pushing you further than you've been before. I could say it's a test of your trust."

I nodded, waiting.

"It is all those things. But it's also a treat for you. Blake is your type, isn't he?"

The scarlet blush rose from my chest to my face, lighting me up with heat.

"You've never said it. But I've seen the way you get turned on when you read about a woman with more than one guy. I know how you get when I use more than one toy on you."

As he ran his hands up and down my arms, I realized Wayne knew me much better than I knew myself. Had the way I looked at Blake really been that obvious?

"You've never been into threesomes," I pointed out, shifting the attention from my actions to his. Wayne said nothing, and by doing so he acknowledged that he wouldn't let the conversation waver from the point. He kissed my shoulder one more time before he stood up from the bed. From the look in his eyes, I knew the discussion was over.

He left the room and when he returned, Blake was with him.

Wayne looked pointedly at the quilt I had pulled up over my body. Understanding what he wanted, I let it fall to the bed. My nipples immediately hardened.

Blake took a deep breath as he looked at me. I studiously met his eyes, unwilling to look lower, though every part of me wanted to see just how excited he really was. Out of the corner of my eye, I saw the slow grin on Wayne's face. He settled against the dresser and watched as Blake and I faced each other over the ten feet that separated us.

"You're beautiful," Blake finally said, and the blush that heated my face seemed to go all through my body and settle between my thighs.

My hand trembled when I reached out toward Blake. He stepped forward to take it. I looked back at Wayne, and he slowly nodded his head. In his eyes was an expression I couldn't even begin to read.

I pulled Blake onto the bed with me.

It was the strangest feeling, to have an unfamiliar man's body in bed with me. Blake was taller than Wayne. Where Wayne was stocky and muscular, Blake was leaner. Where Wayne had straight, short hair, Blake had curls that wrapped around my fingers as I pulled him down to kiss me.

Blake whispered something against my lips. It sounded like "Are you sure?" I kissed him deeply enough to leave no doubt that I was sure. It wasn't just about pleasing Wayne, though that was part of it—I wanted to please Blake, too.

Wayne abruptly pushed away from the dresser and came to the bed. He stood beside it and looked down at me. I met his eyes while Blake kissed a trail down my throat. Wayne didn't say a word. When Blake's tongue found my nipple, I let out a moan. Only then did Wayne blink and tear his gaze away from my face.

Then Blake was sliding his hand between my legs, and suddenly Wayne was the last thing on my mind. I arched up to him and silently begged for more.

"Tell me what you like," Blake said. I did better than that—I showed him. When I put my hand over his and taught him how to make me weak with pleasure, Blake paid attention. Soon he was doing it all himself, rising above me on the bed, looking down at my body as I lost myself in what he was doing. He kept it up, moving his hand in a steady, deep rhythm. The familiar tightening felt almost foreign this time, and I suddenly realized it was because a different man was doing the things that drove me wild.

I was staring at my husband when Blake made me come.

"Good girl," Wayne whispered.

Blake's cock was hard against my thigh. I reached for the buttons of his shirt. Together we pulled it off. When I unbuttoned his jeans, I was very aware of Wayne watching. I pushed the jeans down. The boxers underneath them hid nothing at all. Blake groaned from deep in his throat when I circled my hand around his dick and slowly stroked him.

"You're so damn good at this," Blake murmured into my ear.

When he started to move away, I followed him. On my knees, I opened my mouth and licked the head of his cock. Blake shuddered and ran his fingers through my hair. I looked up at him while I took him into my mouth, one slow inch after another.

Wayne's hand on my hip was like a jolt of electricity, making me jump with the surprise of it. He ran his fingertips lightly over my skin. His other hand slid up to my neck. He took my hair in his hand and moved it away, so he could see what I was doing to Blake.

"Do a good job, baby," he encouraged, and I sucked Blake deeper into my mouth.

Wayne's hand rose from my hip and came down, lightly slapping my ass. He did it a second time, then a third, until he had built up a rhythm. Each time his hand came down on my ass, I sucked Blake into my mouth. Between the spanks, I pulled back until he was almost free of my lips. When Wayne sped up, so did I.

"Fuck—fuck, I'm going to come," Blake warned.

Blake thrust into my mouth. I slid my hands up his hips and held him closer, encouraging him to go deeper. His legs trembled. His breathing became ragged. He said my name and then there was nothing but a long, tortured moan as he started to come.

The first shot of come had such force behind it, I almost gagged. Wayne ran his hands into my hair and held me steady. I couldn't back away—I had to take whatever Blake gave me. I sucked hard, swallowed again, and caressed his cock with my tongue until he pulled back with a satisfied sigh.

Wayne suddenly let me go. I fell sideways onto the bed and looked back at him. He was watching me with the tiniest smile on his face. He opened the nightstand drawer and pulled out the paddle.

"Get him hard," Wayne ordered. "Then ride his dick."

I stared at the paddle, then looked back up at Wayne. His face was calm and quiet, but his eyes gave him away—they were burning with desire.

I turned to Blake. He let out a pleased sigh as I began to suck on him again, stroking him to life with my tongue. It didn't take long before he was standing up straight, his erection proud and thick. He went willingly onto his back, and I climbed over him.

Blake tangled his hands in my hair as I kissed his throat. I worked my way over his chest, kissing him everywhere, teasing him down below by rubbing my pussy just over his cock but not letting him inside me. I kept it up until Blake's body was trembling with tension. Only then did I sit back on his cock, sliding him into me with one long, delicious thrust.

Just as I took him all the way in, the paddle came down across my ass. It was a hard, stinging spank. I gasped at the sudden pain of it.

"Fuck him," Wayne said. "Fuck another man while your husband punishes you for it."

Blake pulled me down for a kiss. All the while I was moving up and down on him. Each time I slid all the way down, Wayne spanked me with the paddle.

"Do you want to make him come?" Wayne asked. Blake was sucking on my nipples while I rode his cock. Wayne was spanking me with the paddle every time I came down.

"Yes," I said.

"Do you want him to come inside you?"

"Yes."

"How much are you willing to pay for it?"

I looked over at Wayne. My motion stopped. Blake looked up to see what had caused the sudden shift, and I heard his quiet gasp.

Wayne was holding a leather whip.

He lashed it against his palm. The red mark rose immediately, blossoming on his skin like a flower of pain. Blake's cock twitched inside me, harder than ever.

"Fuck him," Wayne said. "Make it worth every last stripe of this whip on your ass."

I looked back at Blake. His eyes were wide. He reached up to touch my face, brushed the hair back away from my forehead, and softly kissed my mouth. He took my hands in his, holding them tight, holding me steady.

"Fuck me," he whispered against my lips.

I rose up on his dick. Then I slid down, taking him all the way, focusing on the way he stretched me with every stroke. The whip whistled through the air and cracked against my skin, making me cry out. It stung like a line of fire poured across my ass. The second strike whistled down and this time I buried my face in Blake's shoulder. His hands tightened on mine, holding me down for the punishment I was earning with every thrust.

I rode Blake hard. I put all the force I had into the thrusts. Our hips slammed together. I fucked him hard enough to hurt, even while the whip came down again and again across my ass and my thighs. I was giving Blake pleasure, but taking equal pain for doing so. The combination was heady, the most twisted mind fuck Wayne had ever come up with.

Abruptly, Wayne stopped. Before I could turn to look at him, he grabbed my hair in his hand and yanked my head back. "Make him come," he ordered. "Make him come in my wife's cunt."

Blake didn't need much encouragement. He was right on the edge. When I sat straight up and took him as deep as he could go, he cried out with the pleasure of it. Wet heat flooded me as he arched up, pushing his body hard against mine, letting go into me.

When I caught my breath, Wayne was standing beside the bed, waiting. His clothes were gone. He was breathing hard. Blake slid out of me and I moved to face Wayne, silently asking what he wanted.

"Let me see what he did to you," Wayne said. "Lie down. Show me."

I lay down on the bed and spread my legs. Wayne groaned as he looked between them. Then he was on the bed, coming up between my thighs and driving home with one smooth thrust. His fingers found my nipples and he pinched down hard. Blake sat on the edge of the bed, watching with rapt attention as Wayne's cock slid in and out of the same cunt he had just fucked.

"You're going to take my come too, aren't you?"

Wayne squeezed down harder on my nipples. The pain roared through me, bringing tears to my eyes. That was what it took to send Wayne over that final edge. He yelled out with pleasure as he emptied himself into me. When he pulled out, wetness trickled down my thighs. The sensation was delightful enough to make up for the burning pain of my ass. Wayne sat on the bed and looked at me until my breathing calmed.

"You didn't come." I shook my head. "That's all right. Blake will make you come again. Won't you, Blake?"

Both men looked at each other. It was a question, but the tone of it was more like a demand. I immediately recognized the situation for what it was—if Blake was going to be a play-mate for his wife, Wayne wanted to make sure he still had the upper hand.

Blake picked up the whip. He touched the tip of it as he looked it over. Then he slid it gently against my thigh, drawing a shiver. He gave me a wicked smile.

"Absolutely," he answered.

ABOUT THE
AUTHORS

LISETTE ASHTON is a UK author who has published more than two dozen erotic novels and countless short stories. Writing principally for Virgin's Nexus imprint, as well as occasionally writing for the CP label Chimera Publishing, Lisette Ashton's stories have been described by reviewers as "no-holds-barred naughtiness" and "good dirty fun."

JOCELYN BRINGAS lives in California. Her stories have appeared in Zane's *Caramel Flava* anthology, and Alison Tyler's *Down and Dirty 2, Naughty Stories from A to Z 4, C Is for Coeds,* and *Got a Minute?* anthologies. Her website is www.flirtingwithobscene.com.

ELIZABETH COLDWELL is the editor of the UK edition of *Forum.* Her short stories have appeared in anthologies including *Best SM Erotica 1* and *2, Best Women's Erotica 2006* and several Black Lace collections.

AMANDA EARL's sexually explicit fiction appears in the anthologies *He's on Top: Erotic Stories of Male Dominance and Female Submission* (Cleis Press), *Iridescence: Sensuous Shades of Lesbian Erotica* (Alyson Books), *Cream: The Best of the Erotica Readers and Writers Association* (Thunder's Mouth Press) and *The Mammoth Book of Best New Erotica, Volumes 5 & 6* (Carroll and Graf).

SHANNA GERMAIN is a poet by nature, a short-story writer by the skin of her teeth and a novelist in training. Her work has appeared in places like *Best American Erotica 2007, Best Bondage Erotica 2, Best Gay Romance 2008, Caught Looking, Cowboy Lover, He's on Top* and *Mammoth Book of Best New Erotica*. Visit her online at www.shannagermain.com.

Having experienced a tongue clamp firsthand, **DEBRA HYDE** tries never to speak out of turn—or too much. Fortunately, she's free to write at length without penalty. Her short erotic fiction appears in numerous anthologies, most recently *Got a Minute?, Lust: Erotic Fantasies by Women, Hard Road, Easy Riding: Lesbian Biker Erotica*, and the notable *She's on Top/He's on Top* collections. Her erotic novel, *Inequities*, was published as part of the new Neon Books imprint in late 2007. She writes the long-running web-log, Pursed Lips, and creates the occasional podcast, Pursed Lips, Speaking.

STAN KENT is a chameleon-hair-colored former nightclub-owning rocket scientist author of erotic novels who grew up in England and has a firsthand knowledge of the punishment handed out by sexy schoolteachers. Stan has penned nine original, unique and very naughty works including the *Shoe Leather* series. Selections from his books have been featured in the *Best* *of Erotic Writing* Blue Moon collections. Stan has hosted an erotic talk-show night at Hustler Hollywood for the last five years. The *Los Angeles Times* described his monthly performances as "combination moderator and lion tamer." To see samples of his works and his latest hair colors, visit Stan at www.StanKent.com or email him at stan@stankent.com.

D. L. KING lives somewhere between the Big Wheel at Coney Island and the Chrysler Building and has a passion for roasted chestnuts sold on the street. Renaissance E books recently published King's first novel, *The Melinoe Project*. Please visit the author's website at www.dlkingerotica.com. Send any praise or stray thoughts you might have to dlkinger@dlkingerotica.com.

NIKKI MAGENNIS lives, loves and works in the city of Glasgow, Scotland. After training as an artist, she accidentally fell into writing erotica, and is having a marvelous time. Her first novel, *Circus Excite,* was published by Black Lace in 2006, and you can find her short stories in various anthologies, including the *Wicked Words* series and Cleis's alphabet books *E Is for Exotic* and *F Is for Fetish.*

SOMMER MARSDEN's work has appeared in numerous online publications including Clean Sheets, For the Girls, Ruthie's Club, and The Erotic Woman. Print credits include *The MILF Anthology, Justus Roux's Erotic Tales 2, Sultry Shades of Christmas* and *Five Minute Fantasies 3.* She can be reached at SmutGirl. blogspot.com or www.myspace.com/sommermarsden.

GWEN MASTERS has been accused of writing even in her sleep, a charge she readily accepts. Her stories have appeared in dozens of places, both in print and online. Gwen hides away in a sleepy Tennessee town, writing naughty novels and working on the century-old mansion she shares with her husband and their two kids. For more information on Gwen and her works, visit her website: www.gwenmasters.net.

KATHRYN O'HALLORAN was once told to write what she knows; despite that, she now writes erotica. She finds the research grueling but she goes at it with guts and determination. She's had short stories published in both online and print journals and is currently working on her first novel.

TERESA NOELLE ROBERTS' erotica has appeared or is forthcoming in *He's on Top, She's on Top, B Is for Bondage, E Is for Exotic, F Is for Fetish, H Is for Hardcore, Chocolate Flava 2, Best Women's Erotica 2004, 2005,* and *2007,* and many other publications. She is also half of the erotica-writing team called Sophie Mouette, author of *Cat Scratch Fever* (Black Lace Books 2006) and numerous short stories.

LISABET SARAI has been writing ever since she learned how to hold a pencil. She is the author of three erotic novels, *Raw Silk, Incognito,* and *Ruby's Rules,* and two short-story collections, *Fire* and *Rough Caress.* She also edited the groundbreaking anthology *Sacred Exchange,* which explores the spiritual aspects of BDSM relationships, and the newly released *Cream: The Best of the Erotica Readers and Writers Association.* Her stories have appeared in more than a dozen print collections. Lisabet also works as a freelance editor, reviews books and films for the Erotica Readers and Writers Association (www.eroticareaders.com), Erotica Revealed (www.eroticarevealed.com) and Sliptongue.com, and is a Celebrity Author at Custom Erotica

Source (www.customeroticasource.com). Visit her website, Lisabet Sarai's Fantasy Factory (www.lisabetsarai.com), for more information and samples of her writing.

DONNA GEORGE STOREY, PHD would never have left academia if she'd met someone like Professor Perkins. Her erotic fiction has appeared in *She's on Top: Erotic Stories of Female Dominance and Male Submission, He's on Top: Erotic Stories of Male Dominance and Female Submission, E Is for Exotic, Love at First Sting, Garden of the Perverse, Sexiest Soles, Taboo, Best American Erotica 2006, Mammoth Book of Best New Erotica 4, 5* and *6,* and *Best Women's Erotica 2005, 2006,* and *2007.* Her novel set in Japan, *Amorous Woman,* is part of Orion's Neon erotica series. Read more of her work at www.DonnaGeorgeStorey.com.

MADDY STUART arrived in New York City from the wilds of western Canada, and spends her days painting and programming computers. Her writing has appeared in *Sexiest Soles: Erotic Stories About Feet and Shoes* and *Secret Slaves: Erotic Stories of Bondage,* both in the *Fetish Chest* series. Read more of Maddy at www.maddystuart.com.

CHELSEA SUMMERS has been writing her award-winning blog, pretty dumb things, for over two years. Her work has been published in the United Kingdom in *Scarlet* magazine, *Young Woman* magazine and in the United States in *Penthouse.* Ms. Summers also contributes to several websites, including Yahoo! and Audible.com. She lives and writes in New York City.

Called a "literary siren" by Good Vibrations, **ALISON TYLER** is naughty and she knows it. She is the author of more than twenty-five explicit novels and the editor of thirty-five erotic anthologies. According to Clean Sheets, "Alison Tyler has introduced readers to some of the hottest contemporary erotica around." Visit www.alisontyler.com for more luscious revelations or myspace.com/alisontyler if you'd like to be her friend.

ABOUT
THE EDITOR

RACHEL KRAMER BUSSEL is a prolific erotica writer, editor, journalist, and blogger. She serves as senior editor at *Penthouse Variations*, hosts In the Flesh Erotic Reading Series, and wrote the popular "Lusty Lady" column for *The Village Voice*. Her books include *Caught Looking: Erotic Tales of Voyeurs and Exhibitionism, Hide and Seek, Crossdressing: Erotic Stories, Best Sex Writing 2008, Rubber Sex, Spanked: Red-Cheeked Erotica, Naughty Spanking Stories from A to Z 1* and *2, First-Timers, Up All Night, Glamour-Girls: Femme/Femme Erotica, Ultimate Undies, Sexiest Soles, Secret Slaves: Erotic Stories of Bondage, Sex and Candy, Dirty Girls, Bedding Down* and the kinky companion volumes *He's on Top: Erotic Stories of Male Dominance and Female Submission* and *She's on Top: Erotic Stories of Female Dominance and Male Submission*, and *Yes, Ma'am: Erotic Stories of Male Submission*, the companion to *Yes, Sir*. Her first novel, *Everything But...*, will be published by Bantam in 2008.

Her writing has been published in over one hundred anthologies, including *Best American Erotica 2004* and *2006, Everything You Know About Sex Is Wrong, Single State of the Union,* and *Desire: Women Write About Wanting,* as well as *AVN, Bust,* Cleansheets.com, *Cosmo UK, Diva,* Huffington Post, Mediabistro.com, Memoirville.com, *New York Post,* Oxygen.com, *Penthouse, Playgirl, Punk Planet, San Francisco Chronicle, Time Out New York* and *Zink.* Rachel has appeared on "The Berman and Berman Show," "Family Business," NY1, "Naked New York," and "In the Life." In her spare time, she hunts down the country's best cupcakes and blogs about them at cupcakestakethecake.blogspot.com. Visit her at www.rachelkramerbussel.com and read more about male dominance and female submission at the *Yes, Sir* blog at yessirbook.wordpress.com.